Organized Murder:
A Medium with a Heart

Book 3

Erica J Whelton

Copyright © 2021 Erica J Whelton

All rights reserved.

The characters and events portrayed in this book are fictitious. Any similarity to real persons, living or dead, is coincidental and not intended by the author.

No part of this book may be reproduced, or stored in a retrieval system, or transmitted in any form or by any means, electronic, mechanical, photocopying, recording, or otherwise, without express written permission of the publisher.

Publisher: Sunseri Design Publishing
ISBN: 978-1-956069-00-6

Printed in the United States of America

To my wonderfully patient husband, I appreciate you picking up my slack around the house, especially for making the potatoes.

Books in this series:

Premedicated Murder (book 1)
Replicated Murder (book 2)
Organized Murder (book 3)
Inherited Murder (book 4)
Crafted Murder (book 5)
Destined Murder (book 6)

Other books by this Author:

Mandy's Story: A Glenn Lake Novel (book 1)
Becca's Story: A Glenn Lake Novel (book 2)
Caroline's Story: A Glenn Lake Novel (book 3)

The Haunting of Anna-Rose (Paranormal Suspense)
Decoding Us (Women's Fiction/Friendship)

Chapter One

~Joanna~

Freshly back from my latest tour, I was taking my adopted daughter, Oakley, to my sister's house for a few hours. I had an important errand I wanted to handle, and it wasn't the type of thing I wanted the baby involved in.

I fully expected to be creating new curse words and ugly crying by the conclusion of this venture. That was not something I could do while caring for my young daughter. Plus, she'd likely be confused and upset by my reaction.

After ending things with Clint, the detective I'd worked with on a few murder cases and dated for a brief moment, it got me thinking about our similarly sad backstories.

Clint had been previously engaged to a fellow police officer. Sadly, she'd died in the line of duty, and he never seemed to get over her. Maybe he felt guilty because he wasn't there to protect her, or maybe it was the heartbreaking loss of her. Perhaps both.

Monica had come to me a few months ago, and our conversation made me realize how much I wanted to reconnect with Ted and have a similar discussion. I had questions I needed answers to, and only he could answer them.

Ted was my husband, who died in a drunk driving accident roughly six years ago. We had only been married for two years when he died, leaving me with heavy debts and far too many questions.

My need for closure is partially what got me seeking to regain my psychic powers after blocking them as a young teenager. Before that, I used to enjoy talking to the spirits. They told me funny stories and jokes, plus I got to speak to my grandmother, who had passed before I was born.

Trying to reconnect with my husband and find a way to make money, I faked my abilities at first, leaning on my research skills to make it as believable as possible. Trying to give everyone happy, loving messages made me popular. It led to my brand name, "A Medium with a Heart."

I hoped that closure would help me finally forgive him, move on, and perhaps let myself meet someone else to get serious about. I hadn't even realized how much that piece of my life was holding me back from more, not until I spoke with Monica.

It was the same reason I'd offered to do a reading between Clint and Monica. It was apparent that she was indirectly holding him back from finding love.

When I had broken things off with him several months ago, he hadn't argued or tried to discuss it or even fight me on breaking up. Nor had he shared why he'd agreed so quickly, but I guessed it had to do with losing his fiancée.

I just knew that I was finally ready to try to find love again. Maybe someone who could not only love me but love my daughter. After all, I'd adopted her to give her love, a home, and other comforts that her biological mom couldn't give her and never had herself.

"So, you're really going to do this?" Audrey asked as she walked me out, bouncing the baby on her hip. Oakley cooed and grabbed her aunt's hair.

"Yep. I've never been to his grave." When we reached my car parked at the curb, I turned to face her. "You know all the drama that followed his death. I don't feel like I got a proper goodbye or that I was able to properly grieve."

"I know. That was a mess. Between his family, the girlfriend, and then finding out about all the debt, it was a nightmare."

I nodded, remembering it as if it were yesterday. "Yeah, insane."

"I don't know how you got through it."

"Pure willpower." I sighed softly. "And, of course, your help."

"That's what sisters do." She smiled.

"Well, I better get going. Thanks again for watching her." I leaned forward to kiss Oakley's head. "Bye, baby girl."

She giggled and babbled something that sounded like bye. She was so close to saying her first word. She chattered all the time. It was just a matter of time before something recognizable tumbled out.

"Always my pleasure," Audrey said.

Hopping in the car, I headed first to the florist to pick up a bouquet of flowers. I had been raised to believe this was respectful, but as I browsed through the arrangements, I had no idea what the proper flower was to take when visiting your lying late husband's gravesite, especially when you hated him. My etiquette training stopped short of saying how to handle this situation.

Did red or pink roses say you're a jackass? I couldn't remember.

After looking through them all, I settled on pink and white lilies mixed with matching roses and a bit of greenery and baby's breath mixed in to finish the look.

"These are too pretty to leave. Maybe I'll keep them myself," I said, taking in the floral smell of them and then setting them on the passenger seat.

Flowers in hand, I continued my journey. It was roughly a thirty-minute drive into Appleton, where his family was from and still lived, so I had plenty of time to think and get lost in the memories, from us dating to our wedding day to the day I found out about all the secrets.

Our wedding had been like a fairy tale. It was one of those days where nothing went wrong, even when the flowers arrived late and then weren't the right color. Or how the caterers were shorthanded and food service was slow. Or when the hem of my dress got caught on one of the bridesmaid's heels and ripped. But none of that mattered because, at the time, I'd thought I had married my best friend. So the rest of the stuff wasn't important.

In the limo after the reception, we laughed at all the things that had gone wrong. But for both of us in that moment, we were together, in love, and now married. We had our whole future planned.

Getting the news of his death was terrible. Finding out about the secrets sent me over the edge. It was one of my worst days. It didn't feel real. We had been planning to start our family once he was back from this trip, but he never returned.

If that wasn't bad enough, before I could process all the betrayal or get him buried, the girlfriend's family came after our insurance for money and tried to take their grief out on me. I was as much a victim as they were, but they didn't see it that way, and with the right lawyer on their side, it had been a nightmare to get it all settled.

To add insult to injury, his family hated me, which seems cliché. Though hate might be a strong word. I was an annoyance, and they'd simply tolerated me to make him happy. He was the golden boy of the family, the family favorite who could do no wrong.

They also had another person in mind for him, so their disapproval was partially because I wasn't her. He didn't care, though. He loved me and said he'd never found her attractive.

"We were raised together since birth. She's like a sister," he told me.

As my grief overtook me, they stepped up and took over all the arrangements. While I was thankful for their help, the assistance came at a price. I had to put up with his mom's snide comments and attitude. I tried to understand that she had lost her son and was grieving just as I was, but it was difficult to remember when she made such hateful comments. I should have been used to it. After all, I was not her choice for her son.

The day we were looking for his burial clothing, she had wanted a specific suit, and it wasn't in his closet. She stomped around our bedroom, throwing things and being snippy.

"You hid it from me, didn't you?" she snapped. "You don't want him to look his best."

She continued her rampage through our house, continuing her stomping and flinging of things around.

"Lydia, I promise I didn't hide it." I continued searching through our closet and the piles of clothes she was slinging at me, thinking we must have missed it. "Maybe he had it at the cleaners, or perhaps it was in the car with him."

"Oh, you would just love that, wouldn't you?"

I remember just staring at her. Loved that my husband was dead? Or that the suit she wanted was missing and it ruined her plans?

I decided not to argue with her because she wasn't worth it, and we would've just ended up going in circles. Unfortunately, this was how she often spoke to me, so sadly, I was used to it.

With all this going on, and at his mom's strong suggestion, I was not in the right frame of mind, so I skipped his funeral. I've felt guilty about it since, but at the time, it felt like the right decision for me.

I'd spent that entire day crying in bed, wishing to see him once more and hating him in the same breath. It was the first time in years I'd wished for my psychic powers back.

Then remembering I was finally free of his family and beyond crushed that we'd never start our own. Each of those thoughts and realizations sent fresh tears down my face. My only comfort now was thinking of my adoptive daughter's angelic face.

As the years ticked on, I just never made it a priority to visit. It never interested me, until now.

My life was on track. I had a good, solid business, plus I'd started the family he and I never got to start. I was out of debt, and with this final step of telling off his headstone, perhaps I'd have my closure.

Pulling into the cemetery now, my stomach did flip-flops. Perhaps this had been a mistake. I exhaled. No turning back now.

I wasn't sure exactly what I was nervous about, but it just felt like such a big step for me: forgiveness, letting go, and moving on. I repeated those words as I drove around the perfectly manicured cemetery to his gravesite.

This was a nice place. I could see why the Murphys picked it. The grass was lush and green. Each headstone was neat and clean. Some had flowers displayed, others had figurines and other mementos.

I pulled up near the path leading to his site. I looked around, noticing many ghosts hanging around, but they weren't who I was here for.

I grabbed the flowers as I hopped out of the car and walked tentatively towards his resting place, fighting my nerves the whole way.

His granite headstone glistened in the sunshine. His name perfectly engraved with his birth date and a cheesy quote under it.

Sorry you didn't see me

It was a version of what could only be called his catchphrase. If it was in person, he'd say, "Glad you got to see me" before he'd leave. It always made me laugh when he'd say it. My response was always, "The pleasure is all yours."

He'd always been a huge jokester with a sarcastic sense of humor, and with his quick wit, he always had a comeback for every scenario. It had been one of the many things I'd found adorable about him. He always made me laugh, even when I didn't want to.

As I stared down at the quote that had been engraved in his neat, boxy handwriting, fond memories ran through my mind. His notes always put a smile on my face. When he'd leave on a trip, he'd hide one or two around the house so that while he was gone, I'd find it. Sometimes he'd text it while on his business trips as his way of saying he wished I was with him.

I always knew it wasn't exclusive to us, but it still felt special and reminded me of him and his big personality. I was the opposite of him in every way.

Introverted and shy, except now when I was on stage. He brought out a side of myself that few got to see. Around him, I had laughed a lot, felt confident and free.

It's strange. As I gazed down, this funny realization washed over me. I wasn't mad any longer. Instead, I felt that same confident, freedom of spirit that I'd always felt when around him.

"Ted, wow, I thought I would be angry being here. I'm not," I said, leaning forward and setting the flowers down. "I came to tell you off, but I'm just not feeling it."

I stood there for a moment, not sure what to do next. I'd thought this trip would take me longer. I had a box full of tissue at the ready for me to cry buckets. Yet here I was, not a tear in sight.

With Audrey not expecting me for another hour or two, maybe I could stop at the new shopping mall on the way home or take myself to lunch. Or perhaps I should just go pick up my baby and go home.

A few minutes ticked by as I fought with my indecision when a movement caught my eye, and then realization hit me.

"Ted?"

"Joanna?" He jumped. "You... you can see me?"

"Yes, I can."

"How?"

"It's a long story."

"I have time," he said with a chuckle.

For no good reason, I hesitated. There was no way to avoid telling him. He was dead, and I could see him, so he knew the secret, just not the details of it.

"Well, I never told you, but when I was a child, I had psychic powers and could speak to the dead. Well, still can, obviously."

"No kidding." He rolled his eyes and laughed. "That's a huge secret to keep from your husband."

"You're one to talk. You had a whole secret life that I knew nothing about. Girlfriends, all that debt."

"Jo, I can explain all of it," he said. "But it's a long story."

"I've got time." I crossed my arms over my chest and stared at him.

"Well," he sighed, "what you don't know is that I worked for Hank Hammersley."

"Hank the Hammer?"

"Yes, and that wasn't my girlfriend. She worked for Hank also, and we were trying to bring in a mark." He paused to judge my reaction. I pursed my lips and nodded. "The debt... that is harder to explain, I guess. I was just trying to support a lifestyle that I thought I should have and took out loans."

"Wait, but if you were working for Hank, where was all the money going? From my understanding, he pays well."

He hung his head and mumbled, "I had a gambling problem and took out loans to support it."

"I'd say you had a gambling problem. More than a quarter of a million dollars' worth of problem," I snarked.

"I know. I'm sorry." He hung his head.

"Why didn't you take out a loan with Hank? I know he does that. I'm sure he would have let you work it off, right?"

"Yes, he does and would have. I was one of his... collectors. I knew his methods for getting his money back, and I didn't want that." He paused and looked at me. "Or for you."

My mouth dropped open at his words. So he had thought of me. All these years, I thought he had been selfishly on a fun trip with a girlfriend. But that only gave me part of the story. I needed more answers.

"Then why were you working for Hank if not to pay off your debts?"

"It started as something exciting out of high school. Who wouldn't want to work for a mob boss? It morphed into a way to support myself away from my parents and then to support you and us."

"Okay." I thought for a moment. "You had a big gambling problem and took out a lot of loans. We could have dealt with that. So why keep it from me?"

"I was embarrassed. It spiraled so quickly, and just as I thought I was going to get it under control, I died."

"You shouldn't have been drinking and driving," I said flatly.

"No, Jo, you don't understand. I was murdered."

As his words sunk in, the world around me started spinning, and everything around me blurred. I stumbled to a nearby bench, leaning over with my head between my knees, trying to focus on my breathing.

After I was finally able to catch my breath and thoughts, I asked, "What the hell, Ted? What are you saying?"

"I was on that trip to run down a skip for Hank. The girl worked for Hank, too, like I said. We had been at this party where the guy was supposed to be." He sighed. "He wasn't there, so we left."

"Then why did her family come after me?" I couldn't process the murder part fully yet. One detail at a time.

"They were crazy and thought there was money, I guess. I really don't know."

As the spinning subsided, I stood to pace, muttering to myself. None of this made sense. He worked for Hank the Hammer, and for the last several months, I had been working with Hank and built what I thought was a relationship with him, and he never told me he knew my husband.

To be fair, I had changed my last name back to my maiden name of Webber after Ted died, so it's possible Hank didn't know that. Still, it didn't tamp down my anger.

Ted stood there watching without saying a word. He seemed to be processing my secret too. I wondered if he had known, would he have come to tell me sooner? I'd have to ask him that later.

"So, I don't understand why you think you were murdered. There was no evidence of that in the police reports."

"As we were leaving the club, some guys followed us. I guess they figured out who we worked for or something. They chased us, trying to run us off the road." He paused. "She died instantly, but they pulled me from the car and beat me, then staged it as if I died in the crash."

"That... I... Didn't the police do an investigation? What about security cameras? And who were these guys?"

"We aren't exactly sure who they were, but they stuck around to give witness statements. Said I was all over the road and barely missed hitting them." He shook his head. "I don't know much else. I didn't stick around to find out more. It was all a lot to process at that moment. I had just died, and honestly, my first thought was you."

"Me?" Again, I was shocked to learn this after my distorted version of the story for so many years.

"Yes, first how sad you'd be. I never wanted to hurt you. But then I also thought of how close I was to getting that big payday. Had I gotten that guy, I could've paid off all my debts. But instead, you had to deal with all of it. I wanted to tell you. I should've been the one to tell you." He ran his hands over his face. "Had I known about your powers, I would have been able to tell you and explain and possibly settle all this sooner."

Well, that answered that. One less thing I'd have to remember to ask him, which was good because we had a lot still to catch up on.

"So, that's the thing, though. I had blocked my powers when I was a child. It just kept getting me in trouble. I only recently got them back."

"What? Seriously?"

"Yeah. I had hoped to get my powers back so I could talk to you, ask you about all of this. It took a while, but I finally did get them back, and now here you are."

He smiled at me. "Well, for what it's worth, I am sorry for everything you had to go through with my death."

"I'm sorry to you as well."

We stood there, an awkward silence between us. I didn't know what he was thinking, but I was trying to process the new reality surrounding his death. My emotions were all over the place.

"What have you been doing this whole time? Just hanging out here?" I asked after a few silent moments.

"Yeah, mostly. I didn't feel like being around my family. I did at first, but they were so depressed. My mother was nearly inconsolable. I just couldn't watch that. It was less depressing to just be here." He gestured around.

"I can understand that." Other spirits had told me this before.

I let my eyes glance around to see others mingling among the headstones. I didn't engage with them, though, as I had my own personal stuff to deal with at the moment. The one I'd been waiting on for so long.

"Wait. If you can see me, talk to me, you can talk to Hank, let him know about my death. If I had to guess who was behind this, I think it was a rival of his. There are two I can think of that could have been behind it."

"No, no. I don't want to get involved," I said. "Besides, it's been six years. Nobody is going to believe it, and is it still relevant?"

"Are you saying I'm not relevant? What, just because I'm dead?"

"No, that's not what I meant." I stammered. "I just meant it's been years, and nobody is looking at this as an active case, let alone murder. It was considered an accident."

"Well, it wasn't an accident. I told you those goons ran us off the road. Hank needs to know that we were taken out. He wouldn't stand for a rival killing his folks."

I had a few things I wanted to say to Hank myself. First, how could he not tell me after all this time that Ted had worked for him?

"Fine, I'll do it." I instantly regretted agreeing to this, but I have to admit, I was curious to see how this would play out. The closure I'd craved for years could be answered if I investigated his death. Accident or murder, I'd know.

"Thank you." He smiled at me. That smile used to make me weak in the knees. Heck, even dead, he had the best smile.

"I need to get going, but come by my house sometime, and we can discuss plans."

"Perfect."

I gave him my address and some basic rules to follow. First, no creeping around in my private spaces, like the bedroom and bathroom. Privacy was rule number one with me.

"And I tell all the spirits I work with, please try to keep visits to 'business hours,' no early morning visits. I have already worked with one that did the early thing. I hated it."

That was Jeremy Landon, the first ghost I worked with after regaining my powers. He asked me to find his murderer, and as strange as it was, I ended up adopting the murderer's daughter. Oakley was the best thing to happen to me in a long time.

"Oh, trust me, I remember you aren't a morning person." He winked.

I gave him a dirty look through my laughter. We settled on a date and time before saying our goodbyes.

"Thanks Jo," he said. "Glad you got to see me."

"The pleasure's all yours," I quipped.

I walked to my car, looking back as I reached it. He waved.

Of all the strange interactions I had with the dead, this was the weirdest yet. Who knew I could so easily forgive my late husband for the harm he had caused?

Chapter Two

~Joanna~

Days after seeing Ted, I was still trying to process what he'd said: murdered and working for Hank. How could I not know? How could he have even more secrets?

When I'd picked up Oakley from Audrey, she'd asked me how it had gone. I was vague with the details, as I wasn't ready to tell her what happened. I didn't even know if I could explain it yet. I'm sure I would tell her at some point because I told her everything. I'd likely ask for her thoughts on this odd situation, but it was my secret for now.

My other secret was hiding in the back of my walk-in closet. I had gotten rid of everything from my brief marriage to Ted, except I kept one plastic tote of pictures, notes, and other small keepsakes. Nobody knew I had this, not even Audrey.

I hadn't opened it in years. Not since I packed it all away only a few months after his death, crying the whole time but feeling oh so empowered after.

Since Oakley was napping and wouldn't be awake for another hour, I decided to open the vault and take a walk down memory lane. So I grabbed a box of tissues and headed for my closet.

Dragging the box from the closet, I sat cross-legged on the floor and braced myself for the barrage of images I was about to see, the words I knew I would read.

Opening the lid, the first picture I saw was from our first weekend trip together. A lump formed in my throat as I looked at our faces from more than ten years ago.

We'd gone several hours away to the beach. It had been the perfect choice. Far enough away from our college friends to feel like we were alone, just the two of us, but close enough we were able to drive.

"We looked so young in this picture." I ran a gentle finger across our faces.

I'd gone shopping and gotten a new bikini and a new sundress. The pale pink floral fabric of the dress had been flowy yet fit my curves perfectly. He could barely keep his hands off of me that night.

I giggled, remembering how sexy and beautiful I felt. He had always made me feel that way.

"Even if I still had that dress, I couldn't wear it now, Chewy," I said to my chocolate lab mix, who was lounging nearby. He lifted his head to look at me. "See?"

I showed him the picture. He smelled it and then flopped back on his side. Clearly, this was not his thing. I laughed a little and then set the photo to the side so I could really dig in.

Picture after picture, memory after memory came back. I didn't fight the tears. It was healing.

"Oh, when we moved into our house."

The red brick 3-bedroom house had seemed like a dream at the time. We had spent several weekends replacing the floors, removing wallpaper, and then painting. Finally, we had taken someone else's dream home and made it our own. It had been perfect for us and the family we had hoped to start there.

Our first fight had occurred one of those weekends. We'd been tired and stressed, which exploded into an argument about our painting techniques. We each had a slightly different method, and both of us insisted our way was the best, most efficient way.

Thinking about it now, it was silly, as most of our fights were. Neither of us had been wrong, and in the end, we had gotten the walls painted. We had rarely fought about anything meaningful. The fights were usually something petty.

One of our most serious fights happened after he had died, and it was all a one-sided fight. Just me yelling into the void, wishing and hoping for answers, and begging for my powers so that I could channel his spirit.

It took me roughly six years from that low point to get my abilities back. It happened randomly after one of my shows. His name had been Jeremy Landon, and he had claimed to have been murdered. He had been a pharmaceutical executive, and his death had been ruled a terrible accident with the possibility that he had committed suicide.

It had been the first time I'd ever helped investigate a murder. It had been scary and exciting. It did turn out to be, in fact, a murder, though as it turned out, it had been accidental. The poisonous cocktail had been meant for someone else.

It had not been what I had expected when I had wished to regain my powers, but it had been interesting and had given my now-friends a different kind of closure and had brought me my sweet, adopted daughter in the process.

"Oh, gosh," I said as I pulled out the first shoebox that held greeting cards he'd given me. Pulling out the first, I ran a thumb over his handwriting on the envelope. Dumplin' was how it was addressed. He knew I hated that nickname, but it had become an inside joke. Anytime he could cause me to roll my eyes, he loved it.

I pulled the card out and was greeted by a cartoon dog declaring I was the best.

"I remember this one." We'd gotten into a silly fight. Probably our most serious, though even it seemed so absurd now. It had been about his mother and his lack of defending me to her. She'd really tried to drive us apart over and over.

She had tried to push him towards Paige Mason. She was the daughter of their best friends. In his mother's eyes, only Paige was good enough for her favorite son.

Inside, he'd written his apology.

My sweet wife,

I'm so sorry for always letting you down. It is just so difficult to be caught in the middle between my mother and my wife.

I choose you and love you so very much. I promise I will try to do better by you.

Your terribly sorry husband

I dabbed at my eyes as a new batch of tears formed. This had been not long before his death. He never had a chance to prove that he would stand up for me against her.

I did believe he meant it, though. He just simply didn't get the chance. His life cut short, either as he said, by being murdered or, as the police reported, in a drunk driving accident. I needed to know.

I picked up another card and another, reading each message. I laughed, I cried, and then laughed some more.

We had a good relationship, a solid marriage, except for possibly the issues with the in-laws. I didn't take it too seriously as I knew people didn't always get along with their spouse's family. Though my own family welcomed him in with open, loving arms, even my mother who could be a touch dramatic and sensitive with change and things that weren't about her. But for some reason, she loved Ted, at least until his death, and then she turned into a rabid badger.

"He was never good enough for you," she had said when it was reported that he had died with another woman. "I just knew something wasn't right. He had been too smooth, too good."

"Mother, you know that's not true. You'd loved him as if he was your own," Audrey had said, defending him and me. "There has to be a good explanation for why he was there with her."

I loved my sister always being on my side. She was one of the reasons I had been able to survive those dark days.

"Try to remember that he loved you so very much, Jo," she said. "No matter what, I believe that."

"Then why was he with someone else? Why all this debt? The lies?"

"There has got to be a reason. The Ted I know, that we both know, was thoughtful, loving."

I knew she was right and why I started my quest to find those answers. There had to be a more reasonable explanation for his behavior.

After all this time, I had some of the answers. But the biggest one now was who could have done this to him? Who could have killed him?

I heard Oakley start to chatter over the baby monitor. Chewy popped up, tail wagging as he darted out of my room and down the hall. His buddy was awake, and he was ready to see her.

I quickly put everything away in the tote, promising myself that I would peek again soon. I wanted to finish looking through our keepsakes.

I'm so glad I did look. It reminded me of our many good times that I had pushed aside, only focusing on the negative around his death. All the lies.

"Hi, baby girl," I said, stepping into Oakley's pink and gold room. "Did you have a good nap?"

She babbled and raised her arms to me. I took her over to the changing table for a fresh diaper. I then carried her into the living room so she could have her bottle.

"Here you go, little one."

She held it while I held her.

"Let me tell you a story. It's about the man I used to love, maybe still do," I told her. "His name was Ted. He would have been a wonderful father. Loving, patient, and a huge jokester."

I thought about all the laughs we had shared.

"He loved a good prank. Nothing harmful, mind you, but funny things like this one time he taped a harmonica to my car's grill. It started making this crazy whistling sound on my way to work one morning. I called him to ask what I should do. He started laughing and told me how to fix it." I smiled, thinking about it.

"He was always silly like that. This other time he put glitter and confetti in a greeting card he'd left me. It exploded when I opened it. I was laughing as I lectured him about the mess. Thankfully, he helped me clean it up, but we found glitter for months and months after. Anytime I see a random piece of glitter, even today, I think of that moment."

She took the bottle out of her mouth for a moment to tell me something. I think it was her disbelief that someone would cause such chaos with a card.

"I know. It was crazy, but he was funny that way. Something unexpected." I smiled at her. "You would have liked him."

I told her a few more stories while she finished up her bottle, and then I let her down to play. I watched her crawl over first to Chewy. She said something to him and then continued to her toys. He wagged his tail as he watched her.

I never left them unsupervised together, but he was always so gentle with her. They had a sweet friendship, and I loved watching them together.

While I watched her play, I decided to do some online research on Ted. Granted, it had been so long, I didn't expect to find much, but maybe the stories or reports from his accident would still be available online.

At the time of his death, I'd been too heartbroken, so I hadn't read any of the news articles, and why should I? I knew he had died. No reason to read about it.

"Okay, little girl, let's see if mommy can find any information on this case."

She babbled her support while chewing on her favorite toy, something called a bumpy ball. Baby toys were so neat. I had so much fun buying them. Our house was starting to resemble a toy store, and she was only seven months old.

I typed in his name and found his obituary and a couple of news stories about the accident. The article that caught my eye, though, was about the woman he had been with.

The first one was about her family announcing that they were suing our insurance and estate. I still don't know how they thought we had money, nor do I completely understand why they came after me. It's not like I had anything to do with their deaths. They should have filed against Hank.

Their statements about Ted and condemning him I could understand. I blamed him as well, but now hearing they both might have been murdered changed my feelings a lot. I wondered what her family would think if they knew. Should I try to find her, find them? I could bring them comfort, but had it done that for me to know? No, no it didn't.

I actually think I felt worse. I didn't want to think about those memories of Ted, of that day, or of her. I wanted to think about all the happy pictures of us that I just looked at the past hour.

"No more of that," I said as I closed the article. Chewy lifted his head. "Sorry, Chewy, I didn't mean to wake you."

He yawned and then laid his head back down with a heavy sigh. *Well, excuse me*, I thought.

I read Ted's obit.

"Loving son, wonderful friend." But no mention of being my husband and no language about survived by me either. I knew his family hadn't liked me, but to completely leave me out of his life, or end of life as it were, I didn't understand. It wasn't like I was to blame for his death, but his mom had never been a fan, so I shouldn't have been surprised. She had told him he would regret it if he married me.

They were a big part of why I changed my last name from Murphy back to Webber. I didn't want to be part of their family without him, though at the time, I didn't know I was left out of the obituary.

It felt like a slap in the face, and it was likely meant that way as well. Lydia had always been a bit on the harsh side when it came to how she treated me and talked to me.

What would she think if she knew about his gambling debt and him working for Hank? I can't imagine that the golden boy of the family would be quite so shiny after that.

I wasn't sad to be done with them, that's for sure. However, if I started digging through his life, I may end up crossing paths with her again. That would definitely open some wounds that I was not looking forward to opening.

Regardless, I pushed deeper into the search results. He had social media when we were married, but I hadn't looked to see if it was still available.

A quick search showed that his family kept it going with memories on special days with pictures. There were lots of messages of "gone too soon" or how much someone missed him. Again, no mention of me.

Nothing in my research showed any connection to Hank, though, which wasn't really a surprise. I had done research on Hank's men before with little to no results. However, it appeared that many of them used an alias, which could explain Ted and perhaps Hank didn't know we were married.

How would I find him if he had been using an alias? I had no idea what he might use. Would it be something like Snake or Cobra or maybe the Enforcer or Executor? I shuddered at the thought of finding a side of him that I really didn't know, possibly a violent side.

He'd never been violent. I rarely heard him raise his voice, never at me, but on occasion in traffic. He was always laughing, joking, and enjoying life. That was Ted. The one I knew. The one I'd loved.

Putting the computer aside, I rubbed my temples. I had a headache forming from my swirling emotions. Not going to focus on that now, so instead, I got down on the floor with Oakley and Chewy. He wagged his tail, and Oakley giggled and crawled into my lap.

While we were on tour, she went from scooting and rolling to crawling full speed. I'm so glad my nanny Janie had been able to travel with us. If she wouldn't have been able to, I wouldn't have had Oakley with me and would've missed seeing her crawl.

We played and sang, mostly I sang, for a bit while I tried to decide what to do about Ted.

"This is a weird one," I said out loud. "I'm not sure if mommy can take on this case."

Though I was a medium, not a detective or private investigator, I became quite good at solving these murder cases.

"Or I guess I'm just curious enough to get the killer to reveal themselves," I said as I tickled her tiny foot, causing her to squirm and giggle.

It was only two cases so far, but it was two that the police hadn't solved. The first had been ruled an accident, and the second had been a serial killer that kept eluding the police.

Oakley grabbed my face and planted a sloppy kiss on my cheek, her version of a kiss anyway, which meant my cheek was now all wet with baby slobber.

"Does that mean you believe in me?"

She smiled and climbed out of my lap, grabbing her bumpy ball again. Watching her, I thought how fast she was growing and changing. Before long, she would be walking and talking, running, and then soon after, she would be off to school. A lump formed in my throat as I thought of kindergarten.

"We need to set up a visit with first mommy soon."

Her bio-mom was in jail awaiting her trial for the murder of three people, including Jeremy Landon, who was Oakley and her half-sister Aspen's father. Cate had kidnapped me at gunpoint and then promptly gone into labor, switching from would-be killer to scared single mom.

I guess childbirth changed her view on the world, and she confessed all her sins, and then in a bizarre twist of fate, she asked me to adopt her daughter. I've heard stranger stories on the evening news, so of course, I said yes without much thought.

My brain switched back to Ted as it often did when I thought about kids. We would've had beautiful children.

I sighed when I thought of my next steps. First, I was going to have to go talk to Hank. I'd like to hear what he thinks about this and find out why he never told me about my late husband working for him.

The last time I was there, though, he'd warned me not to drop in without an appointment, so I'd have to figure that out. Maybe I'd reach out to my buddy Al.

Al was Hank's right-hand man who had rescued me from a serial killer. I had escaped and had been lost in the woods. Al was the one to find me. We had quickly bonded, and the once-silent Al was now one of my favorite friends.

I shot off a text to him. He replied almost instantly with an appointment time. Tomorrow afternoon. Perfect.

Since we had just recently gotten back from our tour, I had given all my employees a break after the tour, including my nanny Janie, so I called Audrey again. She loved being an aunt.

"Hello?"

"Hey sis," I said. "Are you able to watch Oakley tomorrow afternoon?"

"Always," she said. "The boys will be thrilled."

My nephews, Harris and Dylan, were five and two years old. They adored their cousin.

"Thanks so much."

"What are you up to?"

I wavered a bit on whether I'd tell her or not. I knew I would, but was I ready?

"Just going to talk to Hank. Nothing special." I tried to say casually.

"Ooh, are you investigating another murder?" Excitement filled her voice.

"No."

"You're lying. Who is it?" When I hesitated, she blurted, "Spill it, sis!"

"Ugh, how do you always do that?" I asked. "Fine. So, I didn't tell you, but when I was out at the cemetery, I saw Ted."

"What?" She exclaimed. "Ted?"

"Yes, ma'am, and he told me the full story of his death."

"Which is?"

"He was murdered while working for Hank."

"Seriously?"

"Seriously. It's an unbelievable story."

I told her the story as told to me. She was as shocked as I was.

"Jo, that's crazy. How did we, or at least you, not know he worked for Hank?"

"I know. He lived this whole double life which obviously I had found out about after his death, but even that wasn't the truth."

"So crazy, but I knew there had to be more to the story. Remember I said that."

"I know. I remember."

There was some commotion in the background, then the voices of my nephews calling for their mom.

"Oh, I gotta go, but yes, bring the baby by tomorrow anytime. I'll talk to you later."

"Okay, thanks. Later."

It felt good to share this secret with her. She had always been able to help me process my feelings a bit.

Hopefully, Hank would be able to fill me in on some more pieces to this story and maybe a quick resolution to my last six years of being a widow.

Chapter Three

~Joanna~

Uneasiness washed over me as I pulled into the parking lot at Leo's. This is where Hank hung out and did a lot of his business dealings. I knew he had an office building for his more legitimate business, but this gave him a place to have food, drinks, and entertain his lady friends. The bar had great food and better drinks, and if you didn't know that it was their hangout, you could really enjoy yourself.

Walking in, a few eyes turned, and usually this would make me nervous, but today I was greeted by some of Hank's men that I had worked with in the past. We had become friends over the past several months.

Had you told me last year that I would be working with and become friends with this mob, I wouldn't have believed it. Yet here I was.

"Hey Jo," Eddie said, coming over to hug me. "How's it going?"

"All good, Eddie. How are you doing?"

"Can't complain."

Al stepped over and grabbed me up in his massive tree trunk arms, lifting me off the ground for a big bear hug.

"Jo, my friend, it's good to see you," he said as he set me back on the ground.

"It's good to see you too. How's your mom doing?"

"Better. Her surgery was successful, and she's been in good spirits."

"Good to hear. I know you were worried about her."

"Hank's not quite ready to talk to you yet. He said to have a seat at the bar, and Darius will hook you up."

I nodded and took a seat at the bar. Darius came over to take my order. I had met him a few months ago after his girlfriend had been killed by a serial killer. The same one that had been stalking me and then kidnapped me. Thankfully, the killer and his mom who aided him in my kidnapping were behind bars.

"Here ya go," he said, setting my vodka cranberry in front of me.

I wouldn't normally drink this early in the afternoon, but when Hank tells you to have a drink, you do it. Plus, as with many of my conversations with Hank, I felt the need for liquid courage.

"Thanks, Darius." I sipped the drink. "It's good. So, how long have you been bartending?"

"A few weeks after the reading you did with me and Macy. Hank thought it was best I get out of the field for a bit, take a break. He suggested this, and I think it fits." He smiled.

"Oh, nice. I'm glad to hear it."

"Thanks. I think the reading you did helped me a lot. Honestly, I had thought about ending it all back then." He frowned. "But thanks to you, I know she is nearby."

I looked to his right as Macy smiled on. "She sure is, and she and I both are glad you didn't harm yourself."

He smiled and then stepped away to help another customer.

"Thanks, Joanna. I appreciate your help in giving him my messages," Macy said before following Darius to the other side of the bar.

I smiled at her and then glanced around as I nursed my drink. As usual, several of Hank's guys were playing pool, and others were chatting around a high-top table.

The man himself was entertaining a busty red-haired beauty in his favorite booth and looked quite pleased with himself. Al was standing not far away, but he grinned and gave a thumbs-up when he saw me look over.

This was not the same Al that I knew just months ago. He had been serious, never showing emotion, stoic when at his boss's side. Before he rescued me, I'd never heard him utter a word.

Since my rescue, he was affectionate and personable with me, cracking jokes and talking about his family: two special needs, never-married sisters, and an elderly mother who recently had surgery to remove a small tumor. Al took care of them all.

As I was finishing my drink, the redhead left the table, and I was called over. He was brought a scotch on the rocks and a cigar.

"Ms. Joanna, what can I do for you today?" Hank asked. "Is it my mother? Does she want to speak to me?"

He asked me this almost every time I saw him. So far, she hadn't come to me, but I looked around to make sure I hadn't missed her. Sadly, nobody spoke up saying they were her, though many dead people were hanging around. Someday I would have to ask him about her. I felt like maybe there was a story there.

"Not today, Hank." I smiled and shifted. I knew this would be a difficult conversation, and I didn't know how to start.

"Well, then what is it? My lady friend will be back shortly and doesn't like when she doesn't have my full attention."

"Of course, I'll try to be brief." I took a deep breath. "I don't know if you remember my late husband, Ted Murphy? He worked for you several years ago."

"Ted Murphy, hmm?" He thought for a moment. "Yes, yes, I remember him. Heck of a nice guy, excellent collector, bad gambler. What about him?"

"I spoke to him recently, and he claims he was murdered."

"Murdered? No, he was killed in an accident. Drunk driving, if I remember correctly." He looked over his shoulder at Al, who nodded. "Lost a girl in that wreck too. Nicki."

My throat tightened at her name. Even after Ted told me she was not his girlfriend, I still had a negative reaction. Would I always react this way to her?

"Ted says they were run off the road by some guys."

"Run off the road? And who does he think did that?" The doubt was heavy in his voice.

"He wasn't sure who they were, but since he was trying to collect a debt for you, maybe it's connected?"

"Hmm, perhaps. I wouldn't be surprised to find out it was that guy. He was a real imbecile. I had to send another one of mine after him. Got him, but he never did pay me back."

I knew what happened to people who didn't pay Hank back, but I couldn't think about it, or I might get sick right here on his table.

However, I was more caught off guard by him saying he wasn't surprised. I was. Why wasn't he? Especially about Ted working for Hank.

"Why didn't you tell me he worked for you? I've known you for a while, working on other cases together, and you never told me." I snapped, forgetting for a moment exactly who I was talking to.

"Joanna, first of all, I've told you before not to question me." His tone sent chills down my spine. He leaned forward. "You don't know what I do for this town. I do things that you could not even begin to imagine, and it's all to protect the people here. Secondly, I didn't know he was married. I try to stay out of the personal lives of my crew. It makes this job a little bit easier to do."

The threat in his words hung in the air along with the heavy cigar smoke. I didn't know exactly what he meant by protecting the town, but I did know some of his methods. I winced at the thought.

"Ted worked for me, yes. He died in an accident, and that's all you need to know." His emphasis on the word "accident" caused my eyebrows to raise a bit. Did that mean he believed it was murder but just didn't want me to dig into it?

"But..."

"It doesn't matter if he was murdered. It was, what, six, seven years ago," he said, pointing a fat finger in my direction. "Now I'm sorry for your loss, but sadly this is how my business works sometimes. After all this time, his death, whether accident or murder, is irrelevant to me." He waved his hand indifferently.

"But..." I tried again.

His icy expression stopped me from speaking further.

"Now, I've given you warnings before, and we've had a good relationship, so I will let you get away with this outburst this time because of your grief. However, you are trying my patience today, and I just don't have time for that." He looked over to Al.

Al, being the good lackey, stepped forward and grabbed my arm, though not too roughly. I stood, nodded once to Hank, and then walked out on shaky legs, but my head held high.

I was not going to give Hank the satisfaction of thinking he had gotten to me, even if he had. I was amazed that I was able to walk out as steadily as I did.

"I'm sorry, Ms. Joanna, he's the boss," Al said as we stepped out of Leo's.

"It's okay. I know him well enough now to know how this would go, but I had to try."

"For what it's worth, I knew Ted, though not well and never knew he was married, and never suspected he would be married to you. He never mentioned it," he said with a shrug.

"Oh, really?" So he hadn't told anyone here about me, not that I was completely surprised.

"Yeah, but then a lot of us guys don't share our private lives here at work. It sometimes makes it hard to do what we do when we know personal things about each other."

I internally shuddered at his words, or maybe it was his tone. Either way, I knew he was serious as I already knew that they did this. Hearing him say it made it real, and I knew it made sense for them to work this way, but it also made me a little sad for them. Some of my best friends had been made through work, especially the two I worked with now, Micah and Tessa. They were more than employees. They were my friends.

"I understand." I nodded. "Is there anything you can tell me about him? Even a little something that might help me get closure?"

"Not much. I didn't work closely with him. Just remember he was a good collector. Always got the money or the deadbeat." Al nodded, giving me a two-finger salute before stepping back inside.

I guess he was done with our conversation. He might have opened up to me recently in so many ways, but he still was a man of few words.

I hesitated, looking up at the front of Leo's faded gray wood shingles and windowless exterior. Hank had a point. Ted's death might be irrelevant to most, but it wasn't to me. I needed the truth about his life and death for my wellbeing. After spending so many years hating him, this was about forgiveness and closure.

As I drove over to pick up the baby from my sister, I replayed the conversation with Hank. It wasn't much, as he had always been a short, sweet, and to-the-point guy, and of course, he had his lady friend waiting for his attention.

He hadn't given me much to work with, actually nothing, but it was a start, and it solidified that I wanted to see this thing through. I had no idea where to start or how I was going to solve such an old crime.

When I arrived at Audrey's house, I found that both her youngest son, Dylan, and Oakley were both napping.

"Want to have a cup of tea before heading home?" Audrey offered.

"Sure."

As she fixed us tea, she asked, "So, how did it go?"

"About like you might expect. He didn't give me much to go on and really didn't answer my questions."

"What are you going to do?"

"I honestly don't know, but if this is true, I have to know."

"While I support you completely, I am scared for you. Twice now, you have gotten pulled into a murder case, and twice you have been in danger."

"I know."

"I really enjoyed these spirits a lot more when we were kids, and they told us silly jokes or funny stories."

"Me too. Remember Grams' stories? Those were the best."

"Yeah, I loved her stories about Mom and Aunt Susie. They were both so different growing up."

Aunt Susie was our mom's sister and had always been the exact opposite of our mother. She was fun and spunky, good at keeping our secrets growing up. She'd let us run away from our overly sensitive and often dramatic mother. Of course, it wasn't truly running away, but it gave us a break for a day or two.

She was also the best at managing Mom when she got a little too emotional. Like when I told Mom about talking to Grams, she wanted to hold an exorcism. Aunt Susie to the rescue.

It was that day, though, that I blocked my powers and never tried to talk to the dead again. I didn't want to hurt my mother ever. After all, she was my mother, and I loved her. She just had her own quirky personality.

"Well, I don't want to find myself in danger again either, not when I have to think about Oakley and her safety too."

"True. Motherhood changes your thinking on life, that's for sure."

"So very true. I knew it before, but it didn't click until I looked down at her sweet face."

"Whatever you decide to do with this information about Ted, I support you."

"Thanks. Your support always means so much."

We didn't speak again about Ted or his possible murder, but it really meant a lot that my sister believed me and supported me. I just had to figure out what the next step in this would be. Would I ignore it or try to find out if it was true?

Chapter Four

~Joanna~

When I'd reconnected with Ted at the cemetery, we'd agreed to a second meeting, and today was that day. He'd be here any minute, and I was oddly nervous yet a bit excited to see him again. My emotions were still swirling nearly a week later after seeing him.

In just our brief conversation, the truths I thought and feelings I'd felt were replaced with confusion, a bit of shock, and maybe some trepidation as I thought about what to do with this new information. All these years of believing one thing, how could I not be mixed up?

He had told me he was an account manager for a large real estate company. Explaining that his travel and time away were because he had to do site visits, looking at properties out of town, conferences, and attending company meetings. I didn't think to question it as it made sense at the time, and I trusted him.

As usual, I had the baby playing on the floor in the living room, and Chewy was at my feet, not far from either me or Oakley. I was absently watching her, thinking about the next steps for my life, not just the bombshell news that Ted had dropped.

After my last murder investigation, I was considering separating my business from my personal life as much as possible. Until now, I had been able to operate out of my home office, but with the serial killer finding my home so easily, I think it was time to look at other options and keep my private life hidden as much as I could.

To protect my daughter, I would need to really consider doing it.

I looked at her as she practiced sitting up.

"You're doing well, little one."

She looked up at me with a big grin. I returned the smile and then looked back at my computer that was in my lap. I was searching for not only an office space to lease but a new house as well. Unfortunately, this one had too many dark memories now tied to it, which made me sad.

After I dug out of the debt, this had been my symbol to myself of how far I'd come. Widowed at only 26 years old and left with a sizeable debt, not to mention legal fees that piled up quickly, when I'd bought this, it was freedom from all of that.

A new house could be a new symbol, one of security and a new chapter for both Oakley and me, or that's what I was trying to tell myself.

I had found a few that caught my eye, but nothing that spoke to me yet. It was going to be a tough decision. Maybe once I met with the realtor, I would find the one.

"Ahem."

I jumped, nearly dropping my computer. "Oh, Ted. Hi."

"Sorry, I hope this is a good time," he said with a smile before his eyes landed on Oakley. "Whoa, you have a baby?"

"Yeah, I adopted her about seven months ago."

"Wow, congratulations." He watched her a second. "We never had a chance to..."

I knew exactly what he meant. We had been planning to try when he returned from that last trip, but he never made it back. So not only had he died that day, but I thought my one chance at being a mother, at least to his children, had died. Yet here I was doing the motherhood thing. Granted, she wasn't his, but that was okay. She was perfect and mine.

"No, we never did."

He continued to stare at her for another moment before turning his attention back to me.

"So, hmm, sorry, that just caught me off guard. I wasn't expecting you to have a baby." He looked back at Oakley. "She's beautiful, Jo."

"Thanks," I smiled at her. "But that's not why you're here. I guess we should get started."

"Ah, yes." But his eyes didn't lift from the baby. "I've thought about it for a long time. I think it could be one of Hank's rivals." Ted looked at me. "I'm leaning towards one specifically. He was after the same guy, but he's also the scariest of them all."

My blood ran cold, as I knew who he was thinking of. This would not end well if it was him.

"You aren't talking about Cecil Edwards, are you?"

"Yes, that's the guy."

No, not Cecil Edwards. He was worse than Hank "the Hammer" Hammersley. Where Hank was more of a businessman, Cecil was evil, sadistic, cruel. Much like Ted had discussed with the guys beating him as he died, there were tales of him torturing his victims.

"Oh, Ted, that's awful. I can only imagine what you must've gone through if it was him." And even if it wasn't, his death sounded horrible and painful. What a sad, scary way to die.

"Yeah, it was terrible, but if it was, I was one of his first victims. He was only getting started with his business then. It all started with a loan from Hank. A loan he never paid back."

"Hank must have felt so betrayed."

"I'm sure. Of course, I was out by then, so no idea." He paced. "I do know Hank's lost several people to him. After a few, he finally just wrote it off as a debt he'd never collect."

"I didn't know any of this," I said.

I'd heard of Cecil, just like I'd heard of Hank before working with him, but nothing in detail about either. I was only starting to understand more about Hank. I assumed Cecil had similar business dealings, just with more evil means to enforce his "terms."

Loans, funding small businesses, and gambling were Hank's primary sources of income. I believed some of what he did was money laundering, though I had no proof. It was just an assumption based on how much money seemed to flow and how connected he was to so many in town.

"Yeah, so it's going to be difficult at best to get evidence on this guy, but he is illegal as the day is long and dirtier than... well, dirt."

"I don't even know how to go about this or where to start with it."

"You can start with talking to Hank. He has resources to fight. You don't."

"Well, about that, I already talked to him, and he told me, basically, to mind my own business."

"Jo, you should've waited for me. I could help. I had a long relationship with him. I had worked for him since I was seventeen years old."

"Seventeen?" I blurted, scaring Oakley and startling Chewy. He let out a bark which further upset Oakley. "Oh, gosh, baby, I'm sorry."

I picked her up, comforting her. Chewy came over and licked her hand. She giggled and grabbed for his ear. I stopped her just short of reaching it. While he was good-natured, I tried to keep her from doing that, both to protect her in case he snapped and to protect him from having his ear or any part of him pulled by the baby.

"You're a good mom," Ted said with a smile. "I wish we could have had our own."

"Me too." I blinked to keep tears from forming and quickly got back on topic. "I think we'll have to think of how best to handle this without Hank."

We sat in silence for a few minutes. The baby calmed and squirmed in my lap, so I put her back on the floor to play.

"So, any idea of where I should investigate or who I should talk to?"

"Well, since you've already talked with Hank and burned that bridge, we can't start there. What about Al? Does he still work for Hank?"

"He does. We're good friends, actually."

"Oh really? That seems like an odd friendship."

"Yeah, a little."

"Are you going to tell me how you are friends with Hank's right-hand man, or do I have to make up my own story?" He said curtly. It sounded a bit like jealousy, which was ridiculous.

"Wow, no, you don't need to do that. I'll tell you." I hesitated a bit. "A few months ago, I was kidnapped by a serial killer, and Al was the one to find me. We've gotten to know each other as friends only since then."

"You were kidnapped? How the...?"

"Yeah, I think you'd be surprised by a lot of my life since losing you."

He looked down at Oakley. "Yeah, I think I would be."

We silently watched the baby play. She crawled around and then pushed herself into a seated position. She looked over at me and clapped. Ted and I both clapped for her. Obviously, she could only see me.

"Wow, Jo, she's perfect." He squatted down in front of her, though again, she couldn't see him.

"She really is."

He reached towards her but then straightened.

"Well, I better go, but I'll be back soon. I'm going to head over to Leo's and see if I can hear anything there."

"Okay. See you soon."

"See ya soon." He looked at me a moment, then at Oakley, and then back at me with a slight grin. "Thanks, Jo."

After Ted left, I watched Oakley play and, for the millionth time in my life, tried to imagine what our kids would have looked like had we had any. Would they have his dimples and dark eyes? Or would they look more like me with my blue eyes and light brown hair?

I remembered his baby pictures. He had soft curls and chubby cheeks. My hair had always been fairly straight, even as a baby.

If he wouldn't have died, though, and we would have had our own children, I wouldn't have Oakley, and I wouldn't trade her for anything in the world.

I leaned forward and brought her into my lap.

"I love you, baby girl."

I kissed her head. She grabbed my face with one hand and my hair with her other, then proceeded to slobber all over my face. I decided she was better than a hundred imaginary children, you know, the ones I never had and would never have. Though honestly, I already knew that.

I thought about Ted's words. Cecil would not be an easy man to get near. Mostly because I knew so little about him. He was from Buckston like Ted had been.

I only knew a little about that town, not having spent a lot of time there due to Ted's family. So I guess I would have to learn more about it and how to talk to Cecil or someone, anyone that might shed light on this case.

Chapter Five

~Joanna~

After Ted's visit a few days ago, I was stuck on exactly how I would investigate his murder. If it was, in fact, Cecil Edwards, this would be tricky and dangerous. Heck, even if it was someone else and Ted had been murdered, what was to stop them from killing me? I've already put myself in a few dangerous spots this past year. Could I really do it once more?

Cecil clearly knew how to avoid the law, but I didn't know how. Perhaps he had his hands in the pockets of law enforcement or the proper government officials in Buckston, his hometown.

This is how it was for Hank here in Creekview. The police department mostly ignored his activities, and I knew that after working with and briefly dating one of the detectives on the force. I got a good idea of how things worked.

I sighed heavily when I thought of Clint. We had great chemistry, but the timing seemed off for us to be more than friends, and at this point, we were barely that. I was a little sad about that. We hadn't hit it off at first. My first impression of him was that he was arrogant, but I have no idea what he had thought about me back then. What I do know is that he doesn't believe in the medium thing. He thought it was magic or luck.

I hadn't talked to him since the day he and his partner, Terry, came to take my final statement on the serial killer case. We ended our romantic relationship that day and haven't spoken since.

But in all fairness, I went on tour shortly after and had only been back about two weeks. It wasn't like I was avoiding him, and I'm sure I would bump into him around town at some point.

It was yet to be seen how I'd feel when I actually did see him again.

My phone rang, shaking me from my thoughts.

"Hey, Micah."

"Hey, boss. I wanted to see if I could come by to do a quick inventory before we start back to work next week."

"Sure, come on by."

"Great, Josh and I will be over shortly."

While on the road with our tour, we had to halt online sales, selling only what we could ship ahead to each venue. We just didn't have the resources to run an online store full-time. Something we hoped to work on before our next tour, which we hadn't even started to plan out yet. We had time.

Our goal was to do direct shipping from a vendor and not close whenever we couldn't fill orders. It was disappointing to our customers, and frankly, I hated it too.

However, before we did reopen our online store, it made sense for him to inventory and cross-check that everything was in place again.

About thirty minutes later, I heard them pull up.

"Your favorite uncles are here," I said, picking up the baby and then heading to meet them at the door with Chewy right on my heels. "Hey, guys."

"Hey, boss." Micah leaned forward to hug me and then gave the dog a pat on the head.

"Hey, Jo. Give me that sweet cupcake," Josh said, holding his arms out. Oakley giggled and nearly jumped out of my arms to him.

We all laughed.

"I see who the favorite is here," I said.

"That's because she has excellent taste, isn't that right, Ms. Oakie?" Josh teased. She giggled and grabbed his face.

He took her into the living room, and they started playing and chatting.

"Wanna help me, boss?"

I looked over at Josh, who waved me off.

"Yep, I'm in," I said, following him. "I had something to bounce off you anyway."

"Oh yeah? What's up?" he asked as we stepped into the garage where we kept all things Medium with a Heart. We had our tote bags, t-shirts, and all other must-have souvenirs.

At the memory of the man who built all this, my heart beat a little faster. He was the one who kidnapped me and had his mother nearly kidnap my daughter. I wasn't as scared for me, but Oakley had been and always was my main concern. Had I lost her, I wouldn't have been able to live with myself.

"So, you know how I had talked to Monica, Clint's fiancée, a while back?"

"Yeah?"

"Well, it got me thinking about Ted."

"Jo, did you...?" He clapped his hands together.

"I did, and he told me that he was murdered."

Micah exclaimed, "What? Murdered? Does he know by who?"

"He doesn't know, but he has a suspect in mind."

"Who?"

I hesitated to even say the name as if it might summon him.

"Cecil Edwards," I choked out.

"Are you serious?"

"That's what he said."

"Boss, you have to stay out of this one. You can't get involved with Cecil."

"I know, I know. I do, but it's Ted. I have to find out what happened to him."

He screwed up his face, obviously not liking what I said. He didn't say anything else but instead turned to start inventory. I jumped in helping by taking notes so he could focus on counting.

"Okay, this all looks good," he said as we got to the last trinkets. "Thanks for your help."

"Great. You're welcome, and thanks for all you do for me if I haven't mentioned it lately."

He winked and then made a few notes on the inventory list, but neither of us made a move to leave or spoke for a moment.

"And as far as things go with Ted," he finally said, "I'm here for you. Whatever you need, I got your back."

Tears sprang to my eyes. "Thank you. That means a lot."

"This is different from the others, though, huh?"

"Yeah, this time it's personal. My husband is the victim, and I need to know the truth. The real truth about how he died."

"And you believe Ted's story?"

"I do actually, or I want to. That's why I want to do this."

"Even after all you've been through? The Landon case? Donovan?"

I thought about his statement. Yes, both of those I'd been in danger, kidnapped both times. Though Cate hadn't scared me quite as much as Donovan had. He had killed several women just to get to me or to satisfy his desire for me. Or whatever excuse he had given the police. To be honest, I hadn't listened as well as I should have as I'd only just been rescued, and my mind was still foggy.

"Yes, I still want to do it. I have to know."

"Well, then you have my full support."

We headed back into the house to find that Josh was on the floor and Oakley was cracking up at whatever he was doing. I looked over at

Micah. His eyes sparkled as he watched his partner play with my daughter.

"When are you guys going to adopt? I'll give you an excellent reference."

"Soon," he said with a wink.

What did that mean? I didn't get a chance to ask before they were headed out the door. They had a party to get to later, and Oakley and I were going to my parents for dinner.

After they left, Oakley and I had an uneventful evening. We had dinner. Mine was grilled chicken and veggies, while she had sweet potatoes and a bottle. Then playtime before bath and a bedtime story.

"Good night, my sweet girl," I told her as I laid her in the crib.

She said something that sounded like appreciation or declaring her love for her bumpy ball. I would never know.

I went to start a load of laundry and wash the few dishes leftover from dinner. Nothing exciting, but it was the life I enjoyed.

Once the chores were done, I grabbed my laptop and did my favorite thing, more research. What did I hope to find? Maybe a lead, perhaps a clue. Anything to give me a direction to investigate.

I looked up Ted first. Nothing new, obviously, since he wasn't alive to generate an online footprint. I still looked. His family had added more pictures, mostly from his childhood. He had been a cute little boy.

"Our kids would have been so cute," I said to Chewy. Chewy didn't offer a reply, just a look and a yawn.

I dug through the same articles I had previously read about his accident and then his obituary. But at least this time, I was much more prepared for being excluded from it.

Since I knew what was coming, I laughed through my second reading of it. There was nothing super special about it, just a typical obit.

When I was done digging through Ted again, I looked up Cecil Edwards. I knew almost nothing about him, mostly rumors and hearsay.

Just like with Hank and his crew, there was little to find on them. There were a few news articles about some business dealings, but he got off on the charges.

I read the articles, though, to see if they would give me any clues.

"Nothing. Ugh," I said to the void, causing Chewy to shoot me a dirty look. "Sorry, boy. That's probably enough anyway."

I closed the laptop, stretched, and then headed to my bedroom to call it a night, but first a stop to peek in on Oakley. Chewy followed me like usual.

I opened her door as quietly as possible and crept across the room to peer into her crib. She was sleeping so peacefully. She smiled sweetly in her sleep and then sighed softly.

I put my hand over my heart. I could literally watch my sweet baby sleep all night.

Chewy sniffed the air and wagged his tail. He loved her too.

I smiled once more at my sleeping daughter and then tiptoed out.

"Chewy, come on," I whispered.

He looked at the crib and then followed me, and we headed to my room for the night.

I was so thankful every night that we were together and safe. Though if I dug into this case too much, that might not always be the case. It made finding a new house and office feel like a priority that I'd have to remedy soon.

I had already made an appointment with a realtor that would help me with finding an office. That was the first step. Once we had somewhere for the business, I could start the process of buying a new house and selling this one.

The thought of leaving this house, our home, made me sad. I looked around my bedroom. I'd lived here for about two years. It held so many good memories, especially in bringing my daughter home. Keeping her safe, though, was my priority, and we'd make new memories.

As I drifted to sleep, I let myself imagine what she would be like as she grew older. It was a nicer thought than thinking about all the other things in my head right now.

Chapter Six

~Joanna~

I decided that today, I'd drive over to Redlynne to look around. It was about two hours away, give or take. Since I didn't have any plans to investigate the case, just look around, I didn't bother to find a babysitter for Oakley. We'd treat it as a fun mother-daughter day trip that, of course, she wouldn't remember, but that's okay. I would.

I hadn't been to Redlynne in years, so I couldn't remember details about the area and wanted to see the spot where Ted and Nicki died. I wanted to see what businesses were around there and start formulating a plan. Maybe someone in the area might have witnessed it or remembered when it happened. Though I had doubts given how long ago it happened.

Redlynne was a bit larger than Creekview at roughly 300,000 people, give or take, which was about 50,000 more than Creekview. Still larger than our neighboring towns of Buckston, where Ted was originally from, and Appleton, a tourist town with the nature preserve as the main draw. It is where I was lost for a few days after escaping the serial killer.

Redlynne was more urban with a focus on young professionals, while Creekview was more family-focused and suburban-like. We had more parks and walking trails, more family activities and festivals, along with better-rated schools.

Though driving through Redlynne today, I could see the appeal, especially if you were that young single professional. There were lots of wine bars and hip coffee shops. Nothing looked childproof, which was not something I would have thought about a few months ago. I hoped we could find a nice place to have lunch later, and I kept an eye open for a kid-friendly park or maybe a museum we could visit.

Creekview was my home, and the nightlife and trendy scene had never been my thing anyway. I traveled a lot for work, so when I wasn't on tour, I preferred to be home in my quiet neighborhood and town. Plus, with the baby now, it changed my lifestyle even more. I loved being home with her.

I peeked in my rearview mirror at her, but I could only see the car seat. Her soft breathing meant she was sleeping. She was such a good baby for traveling. She'd done amazingly on our tour with her go-with-the-flow personality.

My GPS told me to turn left as I neared my destination. It was only a few blocks to the area where Ted lost his life. My heart ached at the thought of seeing the spot where our lives were changed forever.

As I turned another corner and drove to the end of this block, the scenery started to change, causing me to double-check that my doors were locked. It was less trendy and more industrial, dirtier. I noticed that the people in this part of town looked rougher, and there were fewer of them wandering around. There were fewer and fewer cars here as well.

The GPS voice told me to turn again, and I was finally on the street where the accident took place. I slowed as I took it all in. The police had said around the 3000 block, so I continued driving and checking numbers on the surrounding buildings.

Most of these businesses looked abandoned and long-closed, possibly for years. I pulled over and parked near an empty parking lot.

"I think this is it," I whispered as I scanned the area, knowing I wouldn't see any evidence of the wreck as it had been too long ago, but I still looked with hope of some sign that this was, in fact, the place, aside from the fact the closest building was numbered 3001.

They had also told me it was in front of an old newspaper printing company, and that's where I was sitting. It appeared to have been neglected and vacated for some time as they didn't print newspapers here any longer. The building was crumbling and silent.

I stepped out of the car but stood close by so I could keep an eye on the baby. I glanced around, looking for any hint of something unusual but not really knowing what to look for. I never did in these cases, but somehow a clue would always fall in my lap. I just had to be nosy enough.

I sighed. "Come on, give me something."

Suddenly a flock of pigeons took to the air in the empty lot behind me, causing me to jump. They settled above me on the roof of an old warehouse across from me.

I looked around to see what caused them to be jumpy. I didn't see anything, and except for their quiet coo, there were no other sounds in the immediate area. Though I could hear a low hum of traffic from other streets, none traveled down this one. This gave the area an even eerier vibe.

I peeked in on the baby. She was asleep and looked so peaceful. But she would be awake soon and need to be changed and fed, so I'd have to find somewhere for lunch.

As I tried to decide where to go next, I looked around once more. That's when a shadow moved across one of the windows at the printing company. My gaze froze on that spot as my heart skipped a beat. Had someone been up there? Were they watching me?

"Crap." I hopped in the car, put it in drive, and got the heck out of there.

As I passed the lot next to the printing company, a car came to life and pulled out behind me.

"Damn."

I'd been followed before, so I knew what to do. Get somewhere busy and public quickly. With the baby, I had to be careful and keep her from danger.

"This is just a coincidence," I tried to tell myself. "I'm fine."

I kept a steady, calm pace as I drove back towards the populated area. It was only a few turns, and I was back in the thick of traffic and around a lot of witnesses, just in case. I maneuvered, trying to get as much space between me and the potential tail as possible.

The car managed to stay close but not too close. From my experience, this was the classic bad guy move. Close enough to keep up with me, far enough back so I couldn't see them well.

Peeking in the rearview, it looked like there were two figures in the car, but I couldn't see their faces or any distinguishing features. My focus went back to the task at hand: get somewhere safe and away from this car.

The light in front of me turned yellow. I peeked back as I pulled through the intersection. Thankfully, the car got caught at the light. I breathed a sigh of relief and then turned right at the next block.

A few additional turns for good measure, and then I felt safe, which was good because I could hear Oakley waking. I'd need to stop and get her out.

I asked my car to find a restaurant near me. It suggested several. I followed the directions to the most family-friendly one on the list, checking my rearview the entire drive over.

Pulling into the lot, everything looked clear, no car following me. I parked, unloaded Oakley, and headed inside.

"Hi, welcome to the Grape Leaf. How many?"

"It will just be the two of us, but may I change her before you seat us? We drove up from Creekview."

"Oh, nice. Yes, of course. Restrooms are there." She gestured to the right and behind me a bit.

"Thank you."

The bathroom was large and clean, with two stalls plus a changing table. I wiped the area down before spreading out her changing pad.

"Okay, little girl, let's get you cleaned up."

She babbled and chatted to me through the diaper change.

"Oh, really, well, that is interesting," I answered.

She smiled, obviously happy with my reply.

Next, I had to relieve myself, but as Oakley was too big for her carrier and I didn't think to bring in her stroller, I had to figure out how to pee with her in my lap.

"I should have rethought this."

Somehow, we managed, and I even washed my hands like a pro. I had heard my sister talk about doing things like this all the time. I felt like a veteran mom now.

Back at the hostess desk, she greeted us again and led us to a table near a window.

"Here's the menu. Dana will be your waitress. Thank you."

Dana came over to take my drink order and then went to fill it. I got Oakley settled with her bottle in my lap and then browsed the menu. It was hard to read while a baby hand kept grabbing at it, but I managed to read it enough to pick out something.

"Ready to order?" Dana said as she set down my peach iced tea.

"Yes, can I get the grilled chicken salad?"

"Absolutely, that's my favorite. The lemon vinaigrette is amazing!" she said. "And nothing for little one, right?"

"Nope, I think she's good. Thank you."

She nodded and went to put my order in. While Oakley was working on her bottle, I peeked out the window. I could just barely see my car from here. Good luck that we got seated here, as I wanted to keep an eye on it just in case the follower came back. So far, so good as far as I could tell. Nothing looked out of the ordinary.

Oakley got about halfway through her bottle and then seemed bored with it, much preferring to look around and babble to people nearby. I put her in the highchair with some dry cereal and her bottle close by in case she wanted it again.

With her busy looking around and eating cereal, I finally got to glance around the restaurant myself. It was only about half full. Still early in the lunch service, so maybe it would fill up.

It was simply decorated with maple wood tables and chairs that seated four to six. There were single gerbera daisies in small clear glass vases on each table, which I had to move away from Oakley. The artwork around was geometric abstracts in shades of blues and greens. Elegant and simple, modern and clean.

"So, what do you want to do after lunch?" I asked Oakley.

She smiled and told me her thoughts.

"Oh, shopping? Good choice." Though I wasn't sure if that's what she said, I just made it up. Still, she clapped and laughed as if that was the correct response. I loved our little conversations, and it seemed she did too.

Dana delivered my lunch and a few crackers for Oakley, even though I hadn't ordered them. I thanked her and gave one to the baby. She took it and stared at it before deciding what to do with it: straight into her mouth. She only had a few teeth, but she still made quick work of the first cracker. I gave her two more this time, one for each hand. She took a bite of the first and then the second and then went back and forth between them.

"You're so silly."

We both happily ate our lunch and chatted.

After I ate my lunch, I tried to decide what I should do next. Of course, shopping was always an option, and I'm sure there were cute little boutiques to discover all over the town. So I pulled out my phone and did a search of the area. Anything kid-friendly or at least enough that I could take the little one without her getting too bored.

I found a couple of parks that might work. They had a children's museum, but she was probably still a bit young to fully enjoy that. There was also an aquarium.

"That might be fun. Do you like fish?"

She clapped and giggled.

"Alrighty, let's go there."

I punched in the address to the aquarium, but my curiosity took over, and I decided to do another lap or two past the printing company.

Driving by, I didn't see the silver sedan, so I continued down and then turned back. I slowed as I drove by it the second time, tempted to pull in. I didn't know what I hoped to see or why I was curious about the business, but something drew me to this place.

I stopped at the end of the block, looked in my rearview. No cars following me or even around, and I didn't see any reason to stay.

"Alright, Oakie-girl, ready to see some fish?" I said.

She replied with a laugh and something that might have been yes.

"Well, let's go," I said and then pushed the GPS and followed the directions to the aquarium.

I could investigate this case another day. But now, it was time for my girl.

Chapter Seven

~Joanna~

We had fun at the aquarium the other day. It was a nice place, and Oakley seemed to really have enjoyed herself. I'd have to mention it to Audrey as she might want to take my nephews.

However, I had this nagging feeling about that printing company, so when we had gotten home, I did a search on it to see if I could determine who owns it, thinking I might figure out who had followed me. It was owned and managed by a company called Janssen Property Services. It was a relatively new company, only a few years old.

"That's strange," I said when I didn't see the owner listed. In fact, the company owned several properties around Redlynne and appeared to be growing.

Since I couldn't determine who owned it or who had followed me, I made a mental note that if I ever went back there, I'd be more aware of my surroundings.

For today, I wouldn't think about Ted or his possible murder. Instead, I was starting my search for office space to lease. While I loved having it in my home, which I felt gave it a comfortable home-like feeling for my clients, it was time to move our operations for the safety of my daughter and me.

I'd miss my commute from my bedroom to my home office, as well as my coffee breaks where I could simply walk down the hallway to see Oakley's smiling face or into my own kitchen for a drink or snack. But again, her safety was priority one, and it was a small price to pay for that.

Micah, Tessa, and I were meeting the real estate agent that I'd made an appointment with. She was having us meet her at a few properties. Of course, Oakley would be with Janie for the day, just like any workday.

"So, boss, you really want to do this?" Micah asked as he drove us to the first property to meet the realtor.

"Yes, with all the trouble I've had recently, I think it makes sense."

"I agree, plus your popularity has grown since we started. It's time for a change," Tessa added.

"Exactly," I said. "And while we have that nice setup in the garage, the man who built it will always haunt me."

"He was scary, even before he kidnapped you," Tessa said.

"Really? I had thought he was just a nice, awkward man," I said.

"No, he was creepy, but he did good work," Micah added.

I thought about what they said. I wish they would have voiced this sooner, like before I'd been kidnapped. It could have saved me quite a scary memory and a stay in the hospital.

A few moments later, we pulled up at the first place. A red brick one-story office complex that had multiple businesses in it. We were seeing a four-room suite of offices with a storeroom and bathroom.

"This looks nice," I said as we stepped out of the car.

The outside was nicely landscaped with perfectly sculpted boxwoods and evergreens. The exterior windows looked clean and streak-free.

"Hi, Joanna?" A petite woman with her hair in a tight bun wearing a navy suit stepped from the doorway. "I'm LaDonna."

"Nice to meet you. This is Micah and Tessa."

"Wonderful to meet you all. Let me show you the space."

We followed her into a lobby area. I glanced around, then noted the names of the other tenants. Mostly private practice doctors.

The hallways were painted beige with brown patterned carpeting. Almost no décor in the halls. No artwork. No plants. Only business signs on each door announcing which businesses were inside. Not as homey or comforting as I'd like.

"Okay, this is the one that is empty," LaDonna said as she unlocked the door and swung it open to reveal a small space with swirling jewel-toned carpeting. I wasn't expecting such boldness after the bland hallway. "This would be your waiting area."

Other than the crazy carpet, the space was decent. Empty and clean, enough room for about a dozen chairs and maybe a couple of side tables. To one side was a reception window, and next to it a door. We walked through the door to find the offices. The reception area was open behind the window with a wrap-around counter. There were four doors beyond that.

"This is the bathroom," LaDonna said, gesturing to the left. "Then the storeroom here and then two offices."

We peeked into each space. Unfortunately, the storeroom was not big enough for our needs. We'd need at least two this size or bigger to store all the Medium with a Heart merchandise.

When I first started, I didn't know how popular our products would be, but people liked to have something to remember me or my readings, or perhaps it's a way to still feel connected to their last experience with their loved one. Whatever it was, we always had to order more stock.

Though the offices were nice, this might work better for a physician more than for us.

"It's nice, but not quite right," I said.

"We'd need a little more storage space," Micah added as he scanned that room again.

"Okay, well, I have another that has more storage. It's just a few miles from here."

We followed her over to the next property and then the next. Soon the places started to blur together, so I was glad that Tessa was taking pictures and making notes for us because six hours later, I didn't feel like we would find a space that would work for us.

We had the perfect setup with my house, including custom-made storage. Though that was built for us by a serial killer, it at least worked for our purposes. In addition, we had grown into this space, so it fit like a glove.

I was just anxious to get back to seeing clients. We'd taken an extended break until we could find a space, but it was looking like we might have to start seeing families again before finding the perfect place.

"Well, thanks, LaDonna. We'll let you know what we decide," I told her after we saw the last property of the day.

"Great, and if I come across anymore, I'll let you know."

We parted ways and started to head back to my house.

My phone rang with an unknown number. I hesitated a moment but decided to answer it.

"Hello?"

"Ms. Joanna, hello." It was Hank.

"Hank, hi."

"I heard you were looking for a new office space."

"Um, yeah, how?"

"I have my ways," he said. "I might have something for you. Do you have time to meet me?"

I checked the time. I needed to pick up Oakley soon, but I'd just call Janie to say I'd be a little late. "Yes, where?"

He gave me the address, and I quickly relayed it to Micah. Ten minutes later, he slid the car next to Hank's black SUV. Al stepped out, flashed me a grin and a wink, then opened the back door for Hank.

"Ah, Ms. Joanna, I'm glad you could meet me here," Hank said, extending his hand to take mine. He gave it a slight squeeze before nodding his greeting to Micah and Tessa.

"This is a nice building." I turned to take it all in. It was a dark gray stucco one-story office complex. Blue glass windows and neat bushes lined the front. "You own this?"

"Yes, ma'am, and I think this would be perfect for you. It will offer you security and should have ample space for your business. Let me show you."

We followed him into the lobby area. It was a fairly standard lobby area with a reception desk, bold printed chairs, and generic artwork on the walls.

"Is it furnished?"

"This area is, and there are more chairs in the back offices, a few tables too. Of course, you'll have to supply your own desks, office supplies, and any other personal items you might want."

"Okay."

"This is where security would be stationed during your business hours or as requested." He gestured to a desk not far from the receptionist's desk.

"Private security?"

"Yes, I provide security as part of the lease," he said. "Gotta keep our local celebrity safe."

"I didn't think you'd want to help me after our last meeting."

"Ah, that was nothing. I understand you would be emotional about your husband."

The way he said emotional made it sound negative. Of course, I had strong feelings about finding out my husband might have been murdered. However, I just nodded without responding. I knew him well enough now to not take that comment personally, or at least not too personally.

He showed us through the entire space. First, there was a large storage room with ample space for our products and to bundle everything up for shipments. Next, there was space to have a private waiting room close to where my office would be. Then each area had lots of natural light from the many windows, but with the tint on them, it didn't seem blinding either.

"This is perfect. What do y'all think?" I asked, turning to Micah and Tessa.

"Yeah, boss, this could work."

"Agreed."

"What's the rent and the lease terms?"

"Three thousand a month with security and basic utilities, but you have to supply your own phone service and internet."

"Okay. What about the length of the lease? Is there a minimum?"

"I'd like at least a three-year commitment, but for you, I can be flexible."

I looked at my team. I could easily afford the monthly rent, but it definitely cut into our profits. We currently had no rent and no additional utilities to pay, but we'd already done the math, and this is where we needed to be to stay on budget.

"Thanks, Hank. I think we'll take it." I looked at my team's faces when I said it just in case they changed their votes. But they smiled brightly at me, so it was a go.

"Great. I'll have my secretary, Brianna, send over the contract, and then it's all yours."

"Thanks, Hank."

With that, he got back in his SUV and drove away.

"I hope we didn't just sign a deal with the devil, but it sounded on the up and up," I said as I watched his vehicle head down the road.

"Yeah, I think we're fine, boss."

Only time would tell if this was a good thing or a bad thing, but for now, I could separate my business from home. The next step was finding a new home and hopefully a little anonymity in my private life for myself and my daughter.

Selling this house, my home, was sad, but I did not want to go through what I have over the past year again, especially with regards to the serial killer. I had been so close to losing Oakley, and that scared me more than losing myself. But as I thought numerous times since making this decision, we would make new memories, better memories.

This house was just a place, but home was with Oakley and Chewy. I just had to keep remembering that anytime my anxiety crept up on me.

Chapter Eight

~Joanna~

Yesterday had been a productive day. I honestly hadn't expected to find a place, at least not after visiting so many with LaDonna that I'd lost count. However, I did feel bad not giving her the sale as it was clear that she'd worked hard to research all the properties.

Hank came through for me in the end. Had I known, I would have just started with him.

Either way, it freed up today for being nosy in Buckston. I wanted to go scope out where Cecil's team hung out and get a feel for the vibe over there. I knew very little about the place where my late husband grew up. My experience was limited to his family home and the neighborhood where he grew up.

I wanted to see if Cecil was as much of a part of the fabric of Buckston as Hank was in Creekview.

If my past encounters have taught me anything, I could pretty much talk my way into and out of things, most of the time. Though I suppose I did manage to get into trouble once or twice. Today, however, I was feeling optimistic.

I just hoped I didn't run into any of Ted's family. I hadn't seen them since his death. I wondered if his mom still hated me. Hopefully, I wouldn't find out anytime soon.

Janie had the baby. Chewy was at home, so I let Micah and Tessa know I wouldn't be working.

"Where ya going, boss?" Micah asked when I called him.

"Just got a few errands to run." I hated to lie to him, but I couldn't have him talking me out of this.

"Sounds good."

Carrying a bit of guilt for the lie, I drove the thirty or so minutes over to Buckston. In addition to being where Ted had grown up, it is where Caitlyn had taken me when she'd held me at gunpoint, then she promptly went into labor with Oakley. So I switched from kidnapping victim to labor coach in the most unusual way possible.

I laughed, thinking about it. "It's the most ridiculous story ever."

I still don't know why I agreed to adopt Oakley, but I have not regretted it even one day. She was hands down the best thing that's happened to me.

I drove into the industrial side of Buckston, passing right by the warehouse she'd taken me to as I made my way into town. I peeked over at it as I drove by and tried not to think about the what-ifs.

From the industrial park, I hooked a right on Dixon Drive, down a few miles, then a left onto Main Street. It would take me right to the heart of Buckston.

Unlike Creekview or even Redlynne, Buckston was an industrial-focused town. The restaurants weren't the hip and trendy spots of Redlynne nor the family-oriented ones in Creekview. Instead, they were more focused on feeding the hard-working construction workers, factory workers, and medical community. Not that they didn't enjoy the other types of eateries, but it was about eating good, solid meals between shifts and fast so they could get back to work.

I cruised around the few blocks that made up the main part of town. I hadn't spent much time here as I never needed to. Instead, I took in all the sights.

The mom-and-pop hardware store was packed with work trucks. There was a feed store attached to it. We didn't have feed stores in Creekview, or at least I didn't know of them.

The grocery store looked small, at least it appeared that way from my limited view from the street. Our grocery stores were massive, with more food than you could imagine. Things I didn't even know what they were. This looked like it held just the staples. Nothing more, nothing less.

"Nice," I said, driving by. I might stop in before I left town.

I did another lap around. I wasn't sure what I was looking for, maybe a sign that said "Cecil is here." Perhaps someone in the know could point me in the right direction. I'd have to get out and ask around.

A quick time check showed it wasn't quite lunch, but not really breakfast any longer. Maybe I could stop at a diner for some coffee and perhaps a small bite of something.

I found a retro-looking place with silver siding and bright neon signage. I slid my car into a vacant spot near the door.

"Welcome to Gwen's." The waitress smiled. "For one?"

"Yes, thank you," I said.

I loved her pink beehive-styled hair and hot pink diner uniform with a white apron. She looked like she'd been here for more than forty years.

She led me to a booth with cracked vinyl seating. "What'll you have to drink, hun?"

"Can I get coffee, please?"

"Comin' right up."

I looked over the menu she'd left with me. They had all the classic diner faves, and breakfast was served all day.

I could go for some pancakes, I thought.

As I waited for my coffee, I took a look around the nearly empty space. There were two older men at the counter in a heated debate about politics. A sleepy-looking nurse was yawning in one booth, and across from me, a few booths away, was a solo man reading.

The staff was the waitress and cook. I didn't see any others.

She set the coffee in front of me. "Here ya go. Are you ready to order?"

"Yes. Can I get the short stack with a side of bacon?"

She nodded and then went to put my order in. I heard her yell it back to the cook, and then I watched her check on the other patrons.

I added a sweetener and a splash of cream to my coffee.

I can't remember the last time I had real cream, I thought, as I took a sip.

As I waited, I watched the cars driving back and forth outside the window. I wondered where they were going. Work, home, dropping off a kid at school, or was it already too late for that? Others might be heading to the hospital.

In addition to the many factories, Buckston had a large medical center. Creekview had the basics, but you had to come over here if you needed to see a specialist.

There were a few businesses I could see from here too. A florist, a beauty shop, and a bookstore were right across the street. Then there were a few empty spaces advertising they were for lease.

I couldn't quite see it from here, but I knew from driving around there was a bar to the left, and the grocery store was across the street to the right of my view.

The city hall, police station, and post office were at the end of the block. There was an empty, overgrown park next door to that.

The rest of this block was largely empty. The one over had several mixed-use office buildings with restaurants dotted between. A dry cleaner and a nail salon completed that block.

I couldn't figure out where Cecil might hang out. Hank had Leo's, and if you'd lived there for even a day, you knew where to find him. I wondered if it was the same here with Cecil.

Dorothy, the waitress, came over with my food.

"And here's your pancakes and bacon. Some syrup," she said, setting it all down. "Anything else you need?"

"Hmm, no... Oh, just a quick question, do you know Cecil Edwards?"

She inhaled as her eyes darted to the man sitting alone. They made eye contact, and then he looked at me and then went back to reading. "I... I... yes, but no."

She backed away, going straight behind the counter, looking at me only once before busying herself with cleaning. Such a strange reaction, unless that was him. He didn't say anything and barely reacted to the name.

I shrugged it off as I dug into the hot, fluffy stack. These were heavenly. They were sweet on their own and didn't really need much syrup, but of course, I used a little.

Dorothy gave me a wide berth as she moved around the restaurant. She only stopped by once to refill my coffee but didn't speak.

"Thank you," I mumbled as she scurried away.

I finished my meal, paid, leaving her a large tip, and thanked her for the lovely meal. Once outside, I looked up and down the street, trying to plan my next move.

I decided to walk around the immediate area, staying first on this side of the road. I passed several vacant buildings. There was a bakery, a butcher, and a washeteria that I hadn't seen from the diner. Nothing that seemed like a hangout for the rival organized crime group.

Getting to the end, I crossed the street. First, coming to the grocery. I decided to go inside and see what it was like, maybe grab a few things. Stepping in, I grabbed a handbasket.

The produce was on half of a wall, and while there was a limited selection, it all looked fresher than what we had at my usual store. You could almost smell the freshness of it. First, I grabbed a tomato, a head of lettuce, and a bell pepper. Then, there wasn't much else as it was mostly non-perishable items, like cereals, pasta, canned goods, and then a small dairy section.

Buckston had a separate bakery and butcher, so most people must shop at those for their bread and meats.

I grabbed a jar of spaghetti sauce and some noodles, then made my way to the cashier. It was one man who appeared to be in his late sixties, maybe. Thinning hair, life-worn face, and overalls that had seen better days, but he had a friendly smile and a sweet voice.

"Mornin', ma'am." His name tag said Earl.

"Good morning."

"Haven't seen you before. Just move here?"

"Oh, no, I'm from Creekview. I just was out this way and needed a few items."

"I see." He smiled. "These tomatoes come from my son's farm. Same with the peppers. The lettuce comes from the Steele's farm."

"Oh, nice." Who were the Steeles?

"Alright, little lady, that will be $18.55."

I pulled out a twenty, handing it to him. "You don't happen to know Cecil Edwards, do you?"

His face paled, and his mouth formed an "O," and he stammered out, "Hmm, no...?"

It seemed like a statement but came out as a question.

"You don't?"

He looked around and then shook his head. He reached in the register, quickly counting out my change, then handed me the paper sacks with my groceries.

"Thank you, Earl," I said. He flinched when I said his name and then took a few steps back.

Why was everyone so jumpy in this town at the mention of Cecil's name? I knew he was bad, but I guess he might be even worse than Hank.

Hank might be intimidating and did some shady business, and yes, there were rumors of his enforcement methods when collecting his overdue debts. Still, he was fair, and he did a lot for the community. Food drives, helping people open businesses, and other community outreach. As long as you didn't borrow money or if you did, you paid it back, you'd be fine.

I smiled at Earl as I made my way out the door.

As I stepped outside, I ran right into the man from the diner.

"Oh, gosh, I'm so sorry," I stuttered.

"I should think so," he said. "You should be much more careful. You never know who you might run into."

"Of course, I'm sorry."

Did I just get scolded by a stranger for an accident? Or was that another type of warning?

Shaking it off, I walked back to my car and decided that was enough sleuthing for the day. Except for maybe the delicious pancakes and picking up stuff for my dinner tonight, the rest of the trip had been a bust.

The encounter with the strange man left me a little shaken, and I was more than ready to get back to the safety of my home and familiar surroundings.

I looked over my shoulder to see him standing near the grocery, watching me. He held my gaze as I tried to unlock my car.

Flustered, I fumbled with the door handle but finally got it open. I hopped in my car and left town as quickly as I could. The trip hadn't given me anything new to go on, and I knew zilch about Cecil.

"This is so frustrating," I mumbled to myself as I made my escape from Buckston. "At least I didn't see any of the Murphys."

As I made my way out of town, I watched for any car that might be following me. Thankfully, it looked like I managed to not pick up a tail and made it back to Creekview in record time.

Arriving home, my phone rang. I didn't recognize the number, so I let it go to voicemail. I'd check it later. Probably one of those spam calls about my car's warranty.

I forgot about the voicemail for hours until bedtime.

"You need to mind your own business and stay out of mine," said the deep voice. "Stay out of Redlynne. Stay out of Buckston, and you shouldn't have any trouble."

Cecil Edwards, I assumed, but I didn't know he had connections in Redlynne. I guess he got word of my snooping today. I'd have to be much more careful going forward.

Chapter Nine

~Clint~

Things had been quiet around town over the last few months, but after catching a serial killer, nothing else seemed quite as exciting. We'd had a few domestic issues, a couple of traffic accidents with fatalities, but nothing as gruesome or challenging as the serial killer to investigate or figure out. While I was thankful our town was safe, I was bored.

I sighed heavily just as Terry, my partner, came into my office.

"Troubles?" He settled into my extra chair, his long legs stretching out in front of him.

"Just bored with the same old, same old cases."

"Yeah, but it's nice not to find our citizens dead and then not be able to find the killer."

"True, true. I know I sound ungrateful about the quiet, and don't get me wrong, I'm thankful for it, but you know what I mean, right?"

"Yeah, I get it." He paused. "What about finding a new lady friend? Could be a nice distraction."

I hadn't been seeing anyone since Joanna and I decided to end things and just be friends. I scoffed at the thought. Being just friends was not going to be easy with her.

Since Monica's death, Joanna was the first person I could picture myself with long-term, perhaps for happily ever after. But seeing her in jeopardy twice had caused me to pull back and protect my heart.

Maybe a casual date or a fling was what I needed to get out of this funk. I definitely wasn't ready for anything serious, if ever, again.

"Maybe so. Does Whitney have any friends?" Whitney was Terry's wife. In the past, she'd offered to set me up, but I always turned her down.

"I can ask her, but only if you're going to get serious and not string another one along."

"Hmm."

The phone rang, saving me from having to answer fully.

"Hartley here."

"Clint, it's Joanna."

My heart thumped in my chest.

"Oh, hi. It's been a while. What's up?"

I heard her sigh. "I wasn't sure who to call or how to report this, but... I've been getting some threatening calls."

I grabbed a pen and paper. "Calls? Threatening how?"

Terry sat forward, trying to hear while I took down the details.

"Telling me to mind my own business or I'd regret it."

"Jo, what have you gotten yourself into now?" This is why I had to protect my heart from her.

"Nothing."

"It doesn't sound like nothing if you're getting phone calls."

"Fine. I saw my late husband, Ted, recently, and he told me he was murdered. His death was not an accident. I drove out to Redlynne to see where the accident happened, and I also went out to Buckston."

"And?" Here we go again, I thought as I listened to her story.

"And I ran into two things, I guess. Someone was following me in Redlynne, but luckily I was able to shake them." She paused. "And then I went to Buckston to ask about Cecil Edwards."

I nearly dropped my phone at the name.

"I don't even want to know why you were asking about him, but I have to. Why, Jo?"

"Because Ted named Cecil as a possible suspect."

"Of course. You know how dangerous he is, right?"

"I do, but—"

"Jo, there is no but in this situation. This isn't like with Hank. Hank is a fair guy. Cecil is not. I've seen that firsthand."

"But it's about my husband. Wouldn't you do the same for Monica if... I mean, if you didn't know who or how, right?"

I had to actually think about that for a moment. Monica had been killed in the line of duty, a traffic stop gone wrong. But what if I didn't know that?

"Yeah, I would want to know too." I shook my head and looked at Terry to try to read his thoughts. "How do you keep getting yourself into these situations?"

"Right place, right time?" She joked.

"If you say so. There's not much I can do about a phone call or two, but if you can, document the date, time, duration, and anything else you can about the calls. At this time, that's all I can say."

"Okay." Her voice sounded shaky. I knew she was probably scared after being kidnapped twice this past year.

"And, Jo, please try to stay out of trouble."

She gave a light chuckle as a reply before we ended the call.

"So she thinks her husband was killed and now is getting harassing phone calls?" Terry asked.

"Yeah." I ran my hands over my face. "How does she keep getting into trouble like this?"

"Do you believe her?"

I stared at him for a couple of seconds, trying to decide what I thought. I honestly didn't know if I believed any of this hokum, even having worked with her on two murder cases. It seemed like bad luck to me, and despite what she said, I thought it was the wrong place, the wrong time.

"No, I don't. I don't really believe any of this medium stuff. I think she puts herself in these situations for the publicity."

"Seriously? After the Landon Labs and the Playhouse Killer, you still think that?"

"Don't tell me you believe her?"

"Yeah, I do. At first, I thought it was just parlor tricks for entertainment like you do, but once we got the Landon Labs case solved and the killer behind bars, I became a true believer in the paranormal."

I glared at him. How could such a logical man believe in this hogwash?

"And maybe if you believed, you could have her connect with Monica and finally get some closure, find love, and happiness and all that."

With that, he pushed up from the chair and left me alone with my disbelief and shock at his outburst. Terry was always so even-tempered. I was more of a hothead than he was.

Thinking about it got my temper going, so I headed outside to cool off. Hearing her voice got my pulse racing, and I needed to get this negative energy out. Making my way through the station and out the front door, I looked up and down the street before turning toward the small park located near the courthouse. It should offer the right environment for a distraction.

I made a beeline for the half-mile nature trail that wound around the entire park. In the center of the park was a small lake with piers that went out over the water. The city kept this park immaculate and perfectly landscaped. This time of year, the flowers were blooming, and all the birds and squirrels were active.

Watching them as I walked helped ground me a bit, and with each step, as my temper cooled, my pace slowed so I could take it all in.

I loved Creekview, and that's why I served it. I took pride in my job and tried to ensure the citizens were safe and protected.

I greeted a few people as I made my way around the lake. It was mostly older ladies out for a morning walk. They'd giggle to each other after they passed me.

By the time I got back to the station, my head was clear, my ego was boosted, and my obvious feelings for Joanna once again suppressed to protect my heart.

"Better?" Terry teased when I passed his office.

"Shut up."

"Hey, but seriously, I didn't mean to get under your skin."

I stopped and stepped into the doorway of his office. It was next to mine and an exact copy of it. A broom closet was larger, but it worked for our needs, and at least we weren't still in the bullpen with the others.

"I know, man." I grumbled. "I was thinking about it. Even if he was murdered, it's a six-year-old case. You and I both know that most, if not all, clues will be long gone. This isn't like other cases where we get all the evidence fresh. Also, it took place out of our jurisdiction, so we couldn't do anything about it."

"That's all true, but you know you can always call over there."

"I'm not calling him." My uncle was the Chief of Police in Redlynne. "You know he doesn't like when I call him."

"But maybe he might let you see the file."

"And why would I do that? I'm not all that interested in this case."

"For Joanna."

Chapter Ten

~Joanna~

Oakley and I were having lunch with Al today. I thought he might have some information on Ted and possibly Cecil. Anything to get this case moving forward instead of stalled. Everything I'd done to date had me hitting brick walls. Not that I'd expected it to be easy, but something, anything, would be helpful.

The phone calls were a little unnerving, but to me, they proved he was murdered. I had to find out by whom and why. I was determined to investigate this to the fullest. He deserved that, as well as my forgiveness for all the years of hate and bad-mouthing him.

While we waited for Al, I poured a few pieces of dried cereal in front of Oakley. The cereal kept her busy trying to grasp them and maneuver them into her mouth. When she did it, she'd clap and grin at me.

"You're doing so good, little one." I cheered.

I glanced around the restaurant to see if Al had arrived yet, but I didn't see him. As I scanned the room, I noticed a guy in the corner staring at me. I didn't recognize him at all, but he just watched me and didn't avert his eyes when I caught him looking.

His icy stare caused a chill to run down my spine. I'd feel so much better when Al arrived.

I busied myself with Oakley and tried to keep my mind off the stranger. Though I did peek here and there, he was still watching us. What did he want? What was his problem? If I was a confrontational person, I might have said something to him.

Thankfully, Al finally arrived, and I could stop worrying about being alone.

"Hey, there's my favorite girls." He leaned forward to kiss my cheek and then softly patted the baby's head. She cooed at him. He was one of her favorite people. "How's my baby today?" he asked her.

She babbled away, pointing and gesturing as if telling him her life story. He responded as if he understood her. I smiled, though I was feeling a bit like a third wheel as they had their own conversation.

Their friendship was so sweet. Here was this giant, beefy bodyguard for our local mob boss and my tiny, innocent daughter. It was adorable to watch. But as I'd learned more about him and his family, it was no wonder he was as patient and loving as he was.

"So, Joanna, what's good here?" he finally asked me as Oakley got back to her cereal, her story complete.

"I love their steakhouse salad, and any of the pasta dishes are great."

He nodded and read through the menu.

Our waiter came to take his drink order and see if we were ready. I ordered the salad, and Al ordered pasta with grilled shrimp.

"Well, what did you want to discuss?" Al asked after the waiter left.

"Ted."

"Ah, still thinking about that?"

"Yeah, how could I not? He was my husband, and he's claiming he was murdered." I whispered the last word. My eyes drifted to the man in the corner to see if he was still looking. Thankfully, he was distracted by the waiter bringing him a drink refill.

"Sorry. Yes, I understand that," he said. "But I'm not sure I can help you much. I really didn't work with him, like I said before."

I sighed. "I know. I was just hoping you might have heard something, anything that could help give me a clue to who it might have been."

"Wait. Are you investigating this?" He sat forward.

My cheeks warmed with embarrassment. I knew he would disapprove, but I just had to.

"Yeah," I muttered.

"Jo, you can't do that. This could be extremely dangerous."

"But I have to know."

He ran a hand over his bald head.

"Let me do the leg work for you. I have connections, and that keeps you and little miss safe," he offered.

"Okay." I wasn't going to stop, but it wouldn't hurt to have someone else looking into it as well.

"I know that look. Please don't put yourself in harm's way."

I flashed him a coy smile but didn't get a chance to reply as our food arrived. We focused on eating and small talk. Oakley was finished with her cereal and trying to grab my food, so I gave her a bottle.

As our meal wrapped up, the stranger in the corner stood, gave me one long, final look, and left. I breathed a sigh of relief as I watched the door close behind him. Of course, I was just being paranoid.

Al caught my glance. "What was that about?"

"Oh, nothing. He just gave me the creeps."

He turned and looked at the closed restaurant door. He half stood as if deciding whether he should go after the man. Instead, he looked at me and settled back into his chair.

"See, it's already starting," he said.

"You think he was here for me?"

"Well, I didn't see him, but I would bet money that he was." He looked at the baby. "You really need to be careful. If Ted was killed and you dig in the wrong place, it could put you both in danger. I don't know who this is, but if it's who I think it could be, he is dangerous."

"Cecil?" I whispered.

"Yes," he stoically replied.

"I know you want me to stay out of it, but are there any of the other guys that might have worked with Ted or know more about him? Maybe I could just ask them. They would be people you know and trust, and I just want to learn about my husband."

He looked at me for a moment, working his jaw back and forth, I guess thinking about whether he would give me names. Finally, he sighed.

"Yeah, maybe Matt, Bart, or Trent. I can't remember if Eddie worked with him, but you could ask him too."

"Great." I smiled. "I really just want to know more about Ted. I feel like I didn't know him at all."

I didn't add that maybe one of them would slip up and give me hints about who might have killed Ted and Nicki.

"Just stop by Leo's anytime. One of them is always there."

The waiter brought our check. Al grabbed it, slapping down his credit card.

"On me," he said with a wink.

"You're so sweet. Thanks."

With the bill taken care of, he picked up the baby, and I gathered her bag. He walked us to the car and waited while I strapped her in.

"I'm glad you could meet us for lunch. Thanks." I reached up to hug him.

"My pleasure." He did his signature two-finger salute as he turned toward his car.

I put the car in reverse and looked over my shoulder just as the strange man from earlier stepped behind my car, banging his fist on my trunk. I had to slam on my brake so I didn't roll back and hit him. He moved around to the driver's window.

"You better watch your back. You don't know who you are messing with." He hit the window before running off, disappearing as fast as he'd appeared.

My heart was in my throat. Thankfully, the window didn't break. I looked around to see if Al was still in the parking lot, but it looked like he was gone. Oakley started crying, but I was too scared to get out of the car.

"It's okay, baby. It's okay."

She continued but didn't get louder and seemed to be calming a bit, so I finished backing out and left as quickly as possible. I wanted to put as much distance between that man and us. By the time we were a block or two away, she'd quieted to a soft whimper.

While I was left shaken from the encounter, it solidified my resolve that I was on the right path with this murder thing, even though he didn't say his warning was about Ted. My gut told me it was.

Chapter Eleven

~Joanna~

I pushed Oakley in the swing as I waited for Eddie and Trent to join us. Neither of them wanted Hank to know they were giving me any information. When I'd talked to Eddie on the phone, he'd sounded petrified and whispered through our whole two-minute conversation, even though he said he was at home and not at Leo's.

I didn't mind meeting them here, though. It was close to home, and I could spend time with my daughter. Plus, I was thankful they were both willing to help.

Eddie had helped me when I'd had a break-in a few months ago. I'd never really worked with Trent before, but I knew of him. The guys all called him T. Many of them had nicknames they called each other, but they always introduced themselves to me with their first names.

The other guys on Al's list weren't willing to help for the same reason I was at the park today. Nobody wanted to anger Hank. While he could be fair and wasn't as cruel as Cecil when crossed, nonetheless, his temper was hot and his punishments swift.

A dark SUV drove around and parked. In my experience, this was the classic bad guy car, so I thought for a moment it might be Eddie and Trent, but a mom got out and then unloaded her two young children. They immediately ran toward the slides. The mom looked in our direction and smiled but then followed her children onto the playground equipment.

I couldn't wait until Oakley was old enough to run around. She was growing so fast. I might as well look forward to all the milestones. I smiled at her and then looked around my neighborhood park. It was simple with two climbing structures, several slides, and of course, the swing sets.

Benches were strategically placed so parents could watch their children play or couples could visit. Around the entire area was a nice walking path leading into and out of the neighborhood for easy movement for residents.

Ancient oak trees and tall pines offered enough shade that it was comfortable on a hot day, but you could still feel the warmth of the sun. Seasonal flowers and neatly manicured shrubs were planted around the park in tidy flower beds.

The park was never crowded, but there were always people walking around or families playing on the playground. It gave the whole place life and made it feel safe.

I would miss it when we moved. I hadn't put my house on the market yet. I was waiting until we were settled into the new office, then I'd make a plan for the house. I knew it would be a sad day when I did.

Another dark SUV pulled in a moment or two later, but this time nobody got out. It sat there without movement from the inside, though I could make out a silhouette of someone in the front seat. An icy chill ran through me. I looked at my sweet daughter giggling in the swing and then over at the SUV.

Should I grab her and run? Should I call Eddie or Al? Or maybe I could call Clint?

I didn't have time to decide because Eddie and Trent came toward me from the street side parking. My body relaxed as they got close. At least I wouldn't be alone if something happened. They weren't as big and intimidating as Al, but they weren't innocent-looking either, like Oakley.

My eyes flicked to the parking spot and then back to them. Trent caught my glance and matched it.

"Somethin' wrong?" he asked when he was close enough.

"I don't know." I looked over at the car again. "That's not yours, right?" Though I knew the answer since they'd parked on the street side, I just wanted to confirm.

"Nah, we came in his truck." Eddie nodded toward the street parking where a bright red truck was parked. "How long has that one been here?"

"A few minutes. Nobody's gotten out."

They both eyed the vehicle, looked at each other, and then at me.

"Probably nothin'," Trent said. "Maybe meeting someone here, but the other person hasn't arrived yet."

Eddie nodded his agreement but glanced over once more at the vehicle.

"Well, thanks for meeting me. As I mentioned, I recently found out my late husband worked for Hank. Ted Murphy." I picked up Oakley and sat on a bench nearby. The guys sat at an adjacent one.

"Yeah, I worked with him on several jobs," Trent confirmed.

"I did too," Eddie added.

"I feel like I don't know him at all. I don't even know what to ask or where to start."

"I can tell you he was a good guy. Loyal. Always had your back."

"Agreed. Murph was a good friend. Saved my hide more than once," Eddie said.

"He was thoughtful," I said, remembering the flowers or love notes he'd leave me. Always something sweet or a funny joke to make me smile. "I'm glad he was like that with others too."

"Yeah, this one time, I thought for sure I was gonna die. Cecil's guys had me strung up and were punching the crap out of me. Then in comes Murph, guns blazing."

I cringed at the thought of my sweet, loving husband busting in somewhere "guns blazing," but was glad he'd saved Eddie.

"That's great. I'm glad he did," I finally said. "So was there a lot of trouble between y'all and Cecil?"

"Oh yeah, they're our biggest rival," Trent said. His long legs were stretched out, eyes closed as he soaked up the sunshine.

"Why?" I asked. I didn't fully understand all of this or what they all did. I'd learned bits and pieces over the past year but still didn't know a lot.

"Because our business dealings sometimes overlap."

"They also want properties that Hank owns to grow their business," Eddie said.

"Properties?"

"Yeah, you know how Hank does a lot of property management. That's how he makes most of his money. Cecil caught on to the business formula and does the same."

"Ah, I see," I said.

"Oh, and Cecil also has his own gambling thing going too. Hank hates it," Trent said, sitting up. "Again, more competition."

"Really? But I thought Cecil mostly worked out of Buckston? It's a bigger town, I mean at least geographically speaking, so shouldn't he have enough business in his own city?"

"You'd think so, but it's not enough for ole Cecil," Eddie said.

"Yeah, he wants all the business to himself." Trent rolled his eyes.

"Ted said he had a lot of gambling debt. Do you know if he gambled at Hank's or Cecil's?"

"Murph only gambled with Hank as far as I know. What do you know, T?" Eddie asked.

"Some guys did both. He could have too, but I don't know for sure. Why?"

"He said he thought Cecil might have ordered the hit."

They looked at each other, appearing to have their own unspoken conversation, though neither of them said a word to me about what they were thinking.

About that time, the dark SUV backed out of the spot and slowly rolled past us. Eddie nudged Trent with his boot. Trent turned his head. They both stared at the SUV as it nearly stopped in front of us with only the playground equipment as a barrier. Then after a few seconds of an unseen stare down, it pulled out and made its way down the block without incident.

"Who the hell was that?" Trent said, then looked over at Eddie. "Did you see anyone?"

"Nah, couldn't tell," Eddie said, then turned to me. "We should probably escort you both home and do a security check."

"Agreed," Trent said. "Do you have any other questions about Ted before we head to your place?"

"Um, not right now, but can I reach out again if I think of anything?"

"Of course. Call or text anytime," Eddie said.

I got Oakley strapped into her stroller. Trent hopped in his truck, saying he'd go ahead and start checking my house while Eddie walked with us.

We made small talk on the walk home. Eddie was a talkative guy. Tall and lean with an easy, friendly smile that shone in his dark eyes.

"Do you have a girlfriend, Mr. Eddie?"

"Nah, a few lady friends, but nothing serious."

"That's too bad. You're a sweet and handsome guy."

"Why, Joanna, are you flirting with me?" He flashed his dimpled grin my way, causing my cheeks to warm a bit.

"Ha, no. I just think any lady would be lucky to be with a guy like you."

He chuckled as we walked up my driveway. Trent came from the side of my house to meet us.

"All looks good. Your dog isn't too happy with me being here, but other than that, all clear," he said.

"I really appreciate you checking and Eddie for walking us home."

"Anytime. We gotta keep our best gals safe," Eddie said, gently patting Oakley on the head.

"Plus, Hank and half the town would have our hides," Trent added.

"Well, we don't want that." I laughed. "Thanks again."

They watched us go into the house. I waved as I shut the door, then locked up and turned on my security system. Chewy got a treat for being a good boy, and I breathed a sigh of relief to be safe in the house.

I still didn't have my questions wholly answered, but I felt good knowing a little more about Ted and Cecil. It didn't give me much to go on, though.

I knew the case wasn't going to be straightforward or easy to solve. It was an old case with no real clues to indicate murder. It had been ruled an accident, or at least that's what the official report said.

So where do I go from here? Back to Redlynne or back to Buckston? Do I talk to Hank again? There just wasn't much to go on.

Oh well, I wasn't going to solve this now, and I had to get Oakley changed and down for a nap. Then start packing up for our soon-to-take-place move to our new office.

No rush to solve this now or even soon. This was an investigation to give me answers and no one else, so I could take my time and go at my own pace.

Chapter Twelve

Oakley and I had our first mommy and me music class this morning. I don't know about her, but I was looking forward to it.

"Are you excited, Oakie?" I asked as I buckled her in, double-checking her straps were tight.

She babbled something that could have been yes, or the cure for cancer, or my toes are tasty, as she'd recently learned to get them in her mouth. Still, I took it for excitement.

Kissing her head, I closed her door and moved around to the driver's seat.

"Alright, baby girl, let's go."

As I drove, I sang along with the catchy tunes from the children's radio station that I'd put on to get us in the mood.

I'm so glad nobody in the other cars could hear me. I was getting into it a few times, but Oakley was singing her little heart out in the back seat right along with me.

A few minutes later, I pulled into an empty spot in front of the Little Lamb's Clubhouse that hosted the class. I had no idea what to expect, but I thought it would be good for our bond, plus she could be around other children, which she didn't get to do as much as I'd like.

"Good morning." A bubbly woman greeted us at the door. "Welcome to Little Lamb's Clubhouse. Are you here for mommy and me beginner music?"

"We are. This is Oakley, and I'm Joanna."

"Oh, you're Joanna Webber, the Medium with a Heart." She gushed. "I've seen your group readings a few times. I would so love to make an appointment, but I'm honestly a little scared."

"Scared? Why?" I instantly regretted asking, but too late.

"My last conversation with my mother hadn't gone so well, but that was years ago, and now I own this place. I think she'd be proud."

An older woman stepped forward beside her, indicating she was the mother in question. I hesitated only a moment before deciding to do the impromptu reading.

"Actually, Mia, right?"

"Yes."

"Your mother is here." I nodded to her right. She winced slightly. "She says she's so sorry about your last conversation too, and she's very proud of where you are today."

"Really?" There were tears in Mia's eyes. "She really said that?"

"Yes, she really did." I looked at Mia's mother. "She also says she's so proud of what you've done with Ashton."

"Oh, oh... you wouldn't know that. This must be real." She now had tears streaming down her face. "Ashton is my son. I almost lost custody of him, but he's ten now, and we're solid. He has all As in school and thriving."

"She knows and is so proud of how far you've both come together."

"Losing her was my rock bottom. After that, I knew I didn't have that soft place to land anymore, and I had to get my act together for not only myself but my son."

I smiled and shifted a wiggling Oakley from one hip to the other. We wrapped up the reading with a few I love yous and assurances of her mother being nearby to watch over her.

"Thank you, Joanna. This was amazing." She wiped a tear away and then gestured for me to follow her.

We stepped through a doorway into a large room where soft mats covered the floor, and the walls were brightly colored with a mural of cartoon children playing. It was beautiful. Oakley oohed and pointed at things around the room.

There were five other mothers with children already here. I smiled at a few and took a seat in the circle.

"We're just waiting on two more, and then we'll get started." Mia addressed the room before going back to the front.

Oakley babbled and chattered to a boy next to us. He was a little older than her, maybe.

"Hi, I'm Ellie." His mother introduced herself. "And this is Jaden."

"Hi, Joanna and Oakley."

"Oh, such a sweet name. How old is she?"

"Eight months. How old is Jaden?"

"He's going to be a year old this weekend. I can't believe it. It goes so fast."

"It definitely does," I said as I looked down at my adopted daughter.

It felt like just yesterday that Caitlyn was asking me to adopt her so she'd know where Oakley would be. I kept in touch with Cate the best I could, sending her letters and pictures. We'd visited her twice, but now with her trial starting soon, it would be harder to see her.

She'd likely spend the rest of her life in prison for killing three people. I didn't know which one she'd end up at, but the closest one to us was a little over two hours away. Visits would be more complicated then. I'd need to fit one or two in before she was sentenced and transferred.

Our class started, and it wasn't exactly what I'd expected. It was better. We not only sang songs, but we played games and with musical instruments. Oakley seemed to love it.

As we were leaving, I signed us up for more classes. This was something I'd love to do again.

I buckled Oakley into her seat and then headed over to Poppy's Bistro. We were meeting up with Audrey and my mom for lunch.

I'm not sure why I'd agreed to lunch with my mother. She drove me crazy and tended to make everything about her, always needing to be the center of attention. If she wasn't, she would suddenly become ill. With Oakley in tow, though, she would be in doting grandma mode and didn't act like that, so I was hoping for just a nice lunch.

As usual, the bistro was packed, but I managed to find a parking spot. Looking around, I didn't see either my sister's car or my mom's, so I'd beat them both here.

I unbuckled Oakley and carried her to the door. Just as I started to open it, out stepped my worst nightmare: Lydia and Calvin Murphy.

"What the hell?" I said and then instantly regretted it.

"I could say the same to you," Lydia snapped.

"I'm just surprised to see you out here."

"Having lunch, not that it's any of your business."

"I meant after all this time and in Creekview."

"Hmph, it's a free country. We can have lunch where we want to."

Calvin just flashed an apologetic smile my way. He'd always been sweet to me but was clearly under her thumb and never wanted to upset her. He rarely stood up to her.

"Well, yes, it sure is." I stepped around her and into the restaurant. I had not been mentally prepared to see her after not seeing her in over six years.

She grabbed my arm. "Don't you walk away from me. I have things to say to you."

"Excuse me. Do not grab me. I'm holding my daughter."

"Some stranger's baby from what I've heard."

"Seriously?" I had tears in my eyes, and of course, Oakley started crying. I tried to comfort her and ignore Lydia.

Calvin took her arm and tried to guide her away from me, but she pulled her arm back and came toward me again. At that moment, I saw a familiar face walk up and then step between us. It was Audrey to the rescue.

"Excuse me, Lydia. You have no business touching my sister or raising your voice to her. Now you go with your husband and get out of here."

"And who do you think you are? No better than her." She snapped at Audrey but did let Calvin steer her away from us. He looked back once, mouthing sorry as he did. Lydia shot him a dirty look and then one at me.

I was shaking as I watched them go.

"Are you okay?" Audrey said, putting her arms around a scared Oakley, who was still crying, and me.

"Yeah, yeah. I'm fine. I shouldn't be surprised. She's always been nasty to me, but after all this time, I can't believe she still would be."

I kept rubbing my daughter's back, trying to calm her. Thankfully, she was starting to relax, and I think seeing her favorite aunt helped.

The manager rushed over but was too late to help. He apologized and got us seated.

"Here you go. Away from the front door so our favorite hometown celebrity can put that mess behind her." He smiled at me.

I'd been here a few times, but they never let on that they knew me. Of course, he might remember when Laney's tires were slashed in the parking lot. The police were called, and we'd made a small scene outside.

"Thanks, Carlos," I said, remembering his name from meeting him before.

"We're waiting on one more person. Our mother." Audrey informed him.

"I'll bring her right over when she arrives."

After he left us, I got Oakley settled in with a bottle and some little veggie puffs. She kept looking around, likely for the crazy lady who yelled at us, but she calmed and took her bottle and played with the puffs.

"What was that about with Ted's parents?"

"I honestly don't know. I guess she still hates me."

"She's crazy. Always has been."

"I know. I just wish I hadn't seen her when I have Oakley with me." I touched my baby's arm. She smiled at me.

"She's ridiculous. Put it out of your mind." She looked toward the door. "Besides, you need your strength to get through lunch with mom." She nodded toward the front door.

I looked over to see our mom acting all put out by the front door because she couldn't find us. We could hear her from the far side of the restaurant and over the crowd noise.

Carlos stepped forward to help get her to our table.

"Oh, girls, I couldn't find you and thought maybe I had the wrong day or time or restaurant." Then she plopped with great drama into the chair next to Oakley. "Oh, here is my sweet granddaughter."

Oakley smiled and started telling her all about it, whatever it was. I was so thankful for Oakley taking the focus off me. Unlike my mother, I did not need to be the center of attention. Even when I was on stage, I tried to keep it on the person I was giving the reading to.

Thankfully, with my mom gushing over her only granddaughter, we had a reasonably peaceful lunch and a pleasant visit. Though I wanted to talk to my sister privately, it would have to wait for another day. Maybe over wine. I'd have to set that up with her soon as we were long overdue for an evening of sister bonding.

After an uneventful lunch, in which Mom did behave herself, I went home to pack the rest of the things for our move to the new office. I was surprised at how much I had in my office.

Oakley was tired from her day of adventure, so she slept from the moment I put her in the car, and I expected her to sleep for several hours after we got home.

I took advantage of the time to do some research, okay, maybe snooping, into Lydia and Calvin's lives. For obvious reasons, I hadn't kept in touch and honestly hadn't thought of them until recently.

I typed in their names and waited for the search results to populate. Sadly, I was hugely disappointed. Their social media profiles were all set to private. Most of my usual ways to get information also didn't seem to work.

"Dang." I mumbled. "They're smarter than most."

I tried Ted's siblings, starting with his sister. Profiles secure. His brother was the same. After that, I tried a few other relatives I'd known before finally finding a cousin who wasn't good at the security settings.

"And I come up empty. No wonder this profile is open. Nothing but political memes."

Chewy raised his head and yawned.

"Thanks, Chewy. Your support is appreciated." I quietly laughed.

I typed in Ted's name to see if there was anything new on his profile. His mom had written how happy she was he was free now. Was that about me?

Reading the comments, I wasn't the only one confused by her choice of words. Though I assumed it was meant as free of me. She didn't reply to any of the questions about what her comment meant. Instead, she just added another saying she missed him.

I closed the browser window and then the laptop. "Welp, I guess I got my answer on what Lydia's thinking."

Sort of.

I put the computer down and went to finish my packing before the baby woke. I tried to put all thoughts of Lydia out of my mind and just hoped I didn't run into her again.

Chapter Thirteen

~Joanna~

"That's the last of it, boss," Micah said as he loaded it into the moving truck.

We were moving into our new office space today, and I had mixed feelings about it, especially after walking past my now empty home office. I'd been working out of here for a while, and being at home made life so much easier.

"Great," I said, fighting back a few tears.

I snapped the leash onto Chewy's collar. Oakley was with Janie, but I was going to take Chewy with us. He seemed anxious after Trent had been in the backyard the other day, and since we were the only ones in the new building, I thought it would be okay to take him.

Micah drove the moving truck while Tessa, Chewy, and I followed behind him in her car.

"I can't decide if I'm excited about this move or not," I confessed.

"Same," she said. "But it seems like the right decision, especially after the Playhouse Killer."

"Yep, but I don't want to lose that intimate home-like experience we created for our clients, though."

"They didn't come for that reason, and you know it." She quipped.

I laughed. "Oh, I know, but I liked that about our brand."

She nodded and glanced in the rearview mirror, staring for a full second longer than usual.

"And you're really going to sell your house too?" she said as she glanced in the rearview again. Goosebumps started to form on my arms, but I didn't look or ask her what was happening. I think I was just paranoid and looking for something to be wrong.

"I really am. I hate that I need to, but I have to have a bit more separation of work and home life."

"Makes sense." She looked in her rearview mirror once more and, this time, grimaced.

Curiosity took over, so I peeked in the side view to see what was causing her constant glancing and worried expression. That's when I saw the dark SUV behind us.

"How long has the SUV been behind us?"

"A couple of blocks," she said casually. "Though it has gotten a bit closer now."

"Hm." I looked in the side view again. It backed off a bit as I watched it. "Do you think it's Hank?"

"Could be." She looked back at the car. "What do you think he wants?"

"Maybe he's following us to the new office?"

I sent a text to Al asking if they were behind us, then instantly felt stupid because if he was driving, he wouldn't be able to answer me. However, a moment later, an answer came, causing the hair on the back of my neck to stand on end. I glanced in the side view again.

"It's not them. Al says they're at Leo's having lunch."

"Well, maybe call Josh and ask Micah to take a long way?" she said entirely too calmly, though I shouldn't be surprised. She was usually levelheaded.

I called Josh, and he relayed the message to Micah. We stayed on the phone to stay in touch as we made random turns and doubled back toward my house before then turning again in another unexpected direction.

The SUV stayed right with us without missing a beat.

"Maybe we should call the police or maybe Hank?" Tessa said. "Someone to give us protection and backup if needed?"

"Okay. Hey, Josh, I'm going to call Al, I guess, and see if they can help us out."

"Sounds good. We'll keep driving around. Try to stay behind us as best you can."

We disconnected, and I called Al.

"Hello."

"Al, I need your help. We're being followed, though they haven't engaged with us just yet. I'm sure they're waiting until we're somewhere less populated."

"Where are you?" he asked.

I looked around to see where we were. "Actually, not far from Leo's on Main, near the high school."

"Can you drive here?"

"Yes."

"Great. I'll meet you in the parking lot."

I dialed Josh back and told them to drive to Leo's.

Tessa and I watched the vehicle as we made our way toward Leo's. That's when it started to swerve back and forth in the lane and speed up, then slow down. Suddenly, there was a flash of something in the passenger's hand.

"Was that a gun?" I screeched as I ducked down in my seat.

"I think so, but I'm not sure," Tessa said. She tried to make herself smaller while continuing to drive. Her composure was crumbling into a mild panic.

Thankfully, Leo's became visible in the distance. We were almost safe. Micah pulled in, and we quickly zipped in behind. I could see about a half dozen of Hank's guys standing near the door.

"Yikes," I said.

"They're prepared," Tessa said as she parked.

I looked back just as all hell broke loose. The SUV that had been following us slowed and started shooting. Al and his team returned fire.

Tessa and I sank down as low as we could in her car, screaming. Chewy barked wildly at the back window, pawing, trying to get out. Damn, why had I brought the dog?

There was a squeal of tires, and then everything was quiet. Until I heard the worst possible thing.

"Al's been hit!" Someone yelled.

"Someone call 9-1-1!" Someone else shouted.

"Get him inside!" came another voice.

"Oh no," I said, flying out of the car. "Al!"

I ran across the parking lot to him. Chewy right on my heel. Al was bleeding from his chest, but I couldn't tell exactly where. His eyes were closed, but he was breathing.

"Al, can you hear me? Al!"

His hand moved to touch mine. "I'm here. Are you okay?"

"Yes, yes, I'm okay." Tears started to stream down my face. "Please hang in there."

There was a lot of movement all around us, but I just held his hand, whispering to him. He didn't open his eyes and didn't speak again, but at least he continued to breathe.

After what felt like forever, an ambulance pulled up. They took his vitals, assessed his injury, started first aid on his wound before loading him up on a stretcher and into the ambulance.

"Do you want to ride with him?" One of the paramedics said to me. I guess because I'd been clinging to his hand until the last moment, they assumed we were together. Well, we were. He'd quickly become such an enormous part of my life.

"Yes, can I?"

He nodded. I looked to see where Chewy was. Thankfully, Tessa had his leash in hand. He was barking and lunging toward me, but she held him tight. She nodded for me to go, so I hopped in next to Al.

Al was hooked up to an IV, and someone was trying to stop the bleeding. Thankfully, it slowed and didn't appear close to his heart, but too close for my comfort.

He whispered my name and moved his hand, looking for mine.

"I'm here. I'm right here," I said, taking his cold hand.

It felt like we'd never get to the hospital. Were they taking the longest, bumpiest route possible? Finally, we got there. They pulled him out and wheeled him inside.

"Ma'am, you'll need to stay here." The nurse behind the counter said. I nodded, holding back my tears as I lost my hold of his hand. She passed me a clipboard full of hospital forms. "And can you fill these out for us?"

"Um, sure." I doubted I'd be able to fill out much of this. Even if we'd become quick friends, I'd only known him a few months or so, and there was a lot he still kept private. However, it would give me something to focus on while I waited.

I found a seat against a wall in the quietest area I could find. The ER was bustling with people everywhere, both alive and dead. As usual, I tried not to acknowledge the ghosts so I wouldn't be swarmed. Sadly, I had a feeling that some of these dead people had relatives in this very waiting room, and they weren't even aware their loved one had died yet.

I scanned the forms. I knew Al was short for Alvin but didn't know his last name. I also knew his phone number and occupation, sort of. Maybe I could call, and that's when I realized I didn't have my cell phone or purse with me. I'd run to him and never looked back.

"Well, crap," I mumbled. I tapped the pen on the forms, trying to decide what to do.

"Jo... Hey." Came a deep but familiar voice.

"Oh, Eddie! Thank goodness you're here." That's when I saw Hank as well as Tessa with my purse and a few of Hank's other guys.

"Have you heard anything yet?" Eddie asked as he came to my side.

"No, they just took him back a few minutes ago." I sighed. "I'm on form duty, but I don't know enough of the information."

"I got it," Eddie said, taking it from me and starting to write away. "I'm not just muscle. I'm the paperwork guy for our team." He winked.

Was that a needed skill for them? I suppose so.

"Joanna, how are you?" Hank said, taking the seat on the other side of me. He reached for my hand, holding it tightly.

"I'm okay. Scared, shaken, but okay."

"I'm glad you and your team are at least safe."

"Oh yeah, what happened with Josh and Micah?" I said, looking at Tessa.

"They went on to the office with a few of his guys to unload, and they have Chewy. So they'll drop him off with Audrey and then said they'd head up here. Janie is going to take Oakley over to Audrey too, so you only have one pickup spot."

I nodded and then looked over at Eddie, still filling out the forms. He was flying through them. I also noted he had the neatest handwriting I'd ever seen. Crisp, sharp lines, and easy to read. I was a bit jealous. Mine was chicken scratch.

"There. Done," he said with a click of the pen. "Do you want to take it up there?" He asked me as he slid a medical card with the name Alvin P. Washington on it. Mental note to self on Al's last name.

"Yes, thanks," I said.

I took the clipboard with completed forms on them, then stood on shaky legs and headed to the counter. The nurse took the forms, scanned the medical card, and then asked me to have a seat.

"Someone will be with you shortly."

Shortly turned into four hours. By then, Micah and Josh were here as well as a dozen or so of Hank's team.

"Alvin Washington's family?" a doctor asked, coming from behind the counter.

I had a pang of guilt as we hadn't yet let Al's mother know he'd been shot. We'd have to call her soon. Would Hank do that, or should I? I'd only met her once.

"Here," Hank said, and most of us stood up with him.

"Um, okay. I can't speak here or to all of you. Who is the primary contact for this?" The doctor asked, choosing his words carefully.

"You can speak to the two of us." He motioned to me as he spoke.

The doctor nodded. "Come with me."

We followed him through the secured doors through the busy hallways and into a near-empty room. It almost looked like another waiting area, except with just a few chairs and had a door. He gestured for us to sit.

"How is Al?" I blurted, not being able to wait any longer for an update.

"He's stable at the moment. Out of surgery and resting. He was fortunate that it missed most of the vital organs, just going through his shoulder."

"Can I see him?"

"Soon. I just wanted to let you know that we had to call the police since this was a gunshot wound. We have detectives on the way now to talk to him and you about what happened."

"That's fine. We have nothing to hide," Hank said.

I didn't feel nearly as confident as Hank sounded, and I had a sneaky suspicion that I knew the detectives who would soon arrive. My face blushed at the thought. While I'd talked to Clint on the phone recently, I still hadn't seen him since we ended things.

"Great. I'll have you wait here, and I'll see if they've arrived yet."

When the doctor left, I looked at Hank but didn't trust myself to speak. He didn't offer any words, just nodded once at me and then sat perfectly still. I wished I knew what he was thinking. Was he worried about Al? Was he trying to figure out who the shooter was?

It was at least another twenty minutes before the door opened. In walked the super handsome and sexy Detective Clint Hartley, followed closely by his equally handsome but very married partner, Detective Terry Walden.

"Well, well, well, Joanna. I should have known you were involved in this." Clint scowled. "I thought I warned you to stay out of trouble."

"This wasn't my fault. We were moving to our new office and—"

Hank put up his hand to stop me. "Detectives, what she means is, they were on my property, and three guys in an SUV drove by shooting at us. That's when Al was hit."

"Yes, we saw the damage. Our team is still over there collecting evidence."

"I heard," Hank said.

"Any ideas who they were?" Terry asked.

"None. We didn't get a good enough look, but I have Hacker looking at our security footage to see if it caught anything. He said he'd let me know what he sees."

Hacker? Was that a nickname or his occupation? Possibly both.

"We'll need to see it," Terry said while making a note in his small notepad.

"Of course," Hank said, smooth as silk. He clearly knew how to do this questioning thing while I was ready to cry, throw a tantrum, and spill my guts, though I hadn't done anything wrong.

Other than when they first came in, Clint was mostly silent. We made little eye contact, but it still felt like his eyes were on me the whole time.

"And, Jo, do you think this is at all related to the phone calls you've been getting?" Terry asked.

Hank turned to me, some of his composure slipping when he spoke. "Phone calls. What phone calls?"

I filled Hank in on what had been going on but left out the guy who threatened me after my lunch with Al. Partially because I wasn't sure if he knew I'd had lunch with him. It could be frowned upon.

"And you think this might be related? How?" He directed the question to Clint and Terry.

"Because she always lets her curiosity get the better of her. Always puts herself right in the drama," Clint snapped.

I flinched. That stung a bit.

"This time is different," I said.

"How?" His face reddened.

"It's about my late husband, and if he was murdered, I'd like to know so I can forgive not only him but myself." I could feel tears forming. Hank pulled out a handkerchief and handed it to me, whispering something that I didn't quite catch, but it sounded like it was meant to be comforting.

"It was years ago. Even if it was murder, it's a cold case, and all the evidence is gone. No crime scene. Nothing," Clint said.

"Maybe, but I have to try, and honestly, all I was doing today was trying to move into my new office. I wasn't doing anything wrong." Tears fell, so I dabbed at them softly. Clint turned his back.

Terry reached out his hand. "Jo, I understand, but it is dangerous for you to investigate, especially if he was murdered. You don't know what type of person you're dealing with."

I looked at Hank. I didn't know if the detectives knew that Ted worked for him, but it was on the tip of my tongue to suggest again that Cecil Edwards was behind it all. But of course, they wouldn't believe me, and without proof, there wasn't anything that could be done anyway.

There was a knock at the door. Clint was the closest to it, so he opened it.

"Al is asking for Joanna," a young nurse said.

"Can I go, Detectives?"

"Yes, we'll finish with Hank," Terry said.

I mumbled thanks and followed the nurse down the corridor, through a couple of doors, and a few more long hallways before finally arriving at Al's room.

"Jo!" he said weakly when I stepped in.

"Oh, I'm so happy to see you." I came over to his bedside. "I was so worried. How are you feeling?"

"Like I've been shot." He tried to laugh, but it was more of a moan. "Sorry, pain."

"I'm so very sorry you got hurt. I didn't mean for this to happen. I just didn't know how to shake that car."

"It's not your fault at all. Don't blame yourself."

"I can't help it. You'd be fine if it weren't for me."

"Seriously, Joanna, stop. I've been shot before, and I'll likely be shot again."

"How can you be so calm about this? I was scared nearly to death."

"Lots of pain meds." He pointed to the IV with a laugh.

"Well, I'm so glad you're okay."

At that moment, Hank joined us. Hank filled him in on what the doctor said, the detectives questioning us, and that Hacker had been able to pull some information from the security cameras.

"It looks like that new group."

"The one out of Redlynne?" Al asked.

"Yes, but I don't know much about them yet."

"Not Cecil Edwards?" I asked and then immediately regretted speaking up.

"From what Hacker said, it didn't look like any of Cecil's guys that we're familiar with. Why?"

"Because Ted thought that Cecil's group might have murdered him," I said.

"I really doubt it was Cecil. He was small potatoes back then. He's only come into his own in the past few years or so. Though he's tried to copy my business model for a while and thinks he was big-time before he truly was. Heck, he barely is now." Hank scoffed.

"Well, couldn't it have been one of his first hits?" I was probably grasping at straws, but he was the only named suspect. I had no other leads, except whoever this Redlynne group was, but nobody seemed to know anything about them.

"I suppose, but honestly, he was killed so long ago, and while I know you're upset about it, you need to let it go," Hank said.

He was probably right, but I knew I wouldn't give up, or at least not easily.

We finished up visiting with Al. I promised him I'd check on his mom and sisters until he was out. They depended on him for almost everything, especially his elderly mother.

When Hank and I made it back to the group, he filled them in on Al's condition, and then we all parted ways.

"I'll keep you updated on his progress, Jo," Hank said. "Please take care of yourself and that little princess of yours. Remember what I said about your husband."

Tessa had waited and was able to drive me to Audrey's and then home.

"You gonna be okay alone tonight?" she asked as she parked in my driveway.

"Hm, yeah. We'll be fine." But honestly, I wasn't sure. I was so worried about Al and about who was after me. "But do you want to stay for dinner?"

"Yes, let me just let my mom know." She hit dial on her phone while I got Oakley and Chewy into the house.

"Mom says she's bringing over dinner."

Ms. Ruby's cooking was fabulous, so I couldn't wait for her to get here with food.

I got Oakley in and settled in the living room with her toys. Chewy wanted to go in the backyard. While I did that, Tessa made herself at home, fixing us both drinks and settling in front of the television as well as keeping an eye on Oakley for me.

"Crazy day," I said, joining her.

"So crazy. Any ideas on who?"

"None, but Hank said his guy thought it was a group out of Redlynne."

"But they don't know for sure?"

"No." I closed my eyes as I could feel tears start to form. "I just feel awful about Al."

Tessa nodded.

We changed the subject as we waited for Ruby. Thankfully, she arrived shortly after, loaded down with all kinds of yummy-smelling food, and she brought along Tessa's brother, Levi, and her sister, Elsa.

"Hey, Levi, Elsa. I haven't seen y'all in forever." They were twins and three years younger than Tessa.

"Yeah, we're home for a break," Elsa said as she gave me a hug.

"How's college going?" I asked.

"Good," Elsa said.

"It's okay," Levi added.

"Just okay?" I asked. Levi had always been a hard nut to crack and a bit dramatic.

"Don't let him fool you, Jo. He's on the Dean's list and is Mister Popular among the ladies," Ms. Ruby said with a wink.

"The ladies, huh?"

He just shrugged, flashing me a wide grin.

The rest of the evening was uneventful as far as bad guys, but it was wonderful to have Tessa and her family here. It was a nice distraction from the day. I hated to see the night end. It would mean being alone with my thoughts and worry about Al.

"Thank you for the great food and company," I said to Ms. Ruby as I walked them all out hours later.

"You are so welcome, dear. I love sharing my food, and I love you and Oakley." She wrapped me in her arms. "Be safe."

I hugged each of the twins, though with Levi, it was more of me hugging and him leaning on me.

"Are you sure you don't want me to stay with you?" Tessa asked.

I hesitated because it would make me feel better to have someone else here with me, but I hated to inconvenience her.

"Nah, I'll be fine."

"You hesitated," she said. "I'm staying."

To say I was relieved was an understatement. Having her here was going to make the night a lot less stressful.

I would never be able to pay Tessa back for her friendship, but I would sure try.

Chapter Fourteen

~Clint~

After we left the hospital, we headed back over to Leo's to work with Hacker. He'd called while we were still with Hank to say he had good footage of the drive-by.

Along with the forensic department, we'd already collected bullets, photos, and the other evidence we needed from the scene. We'd then left the team to finish up so we could head to the hospital to interview Hank and Joanna.

Now on the way back, I was anxious to see this footage. Hank hadn't caused us trouble in a while, but seeing that Joanna was involved hadn't surprised me.

My blood was still boiling that she'd once again put herself in the middle of a dangerous situation. It was moments like this that I didn't regret ending our relationship. Had things gone much further with us and something happened to her, I would never forgive myself.

My heart still hurt when I thought of Monica and losing her. She'd been taken too young, too soon. But at least she'd been killed in the line of duty and not just chasing some crazy scam or drama.

"Why did you give Joanna such a hard time? She was clearly upset about Al being shot and also being harassed," Terry said, breaking the silence.

"You know why." I know I probably sounded childish, but I was irritated with her and myself for still having feelings for her.

"I know, but I want to hear you say it," he teased.

"Screw you." I slammed my arms across my chest and stared out the window.

"That's my friend." He chuckled at my expense.

I shot him a dirty look as we pulled into Leo's, and I was saved from any further conversation about Joanna. We parked and headed in.

Hacker greeted us at the door. His nickname was earned due to his role as the technical support for Hank. He wasn't a true hacker, or at least that we knew of. He ran all the computer and security equipment for Hank's business and properties.

"Hey, detectives. Glad y'all could come over. I already made you a copy." He handed Terry a USB drive.

"Thanks."

"Y'all want a drink or something?"

"Nah, on the job," Terry said.

"Oh, of course, duh. Water then?"

"None for me," I said.

"Me neither," Terry said.

"Alrighty, follow me, and I'll show you the footage."

He showed us into a back office. It was dark except for the glare from a dozen or so computer monitors that lined one wall. It appeared to be images from their various properties, including here at Leo's.

I watched for a moment, trying to pinpoint where each was. I made a mental note as this could be helpful in future cases.

"Alright, so I have it ready on this one here." He sat at the desk in front of the monitors. He pointed to one of the many screens and then, with a few taps on the mouse, the video started playing. "Okay, so here you see our team come out the door, then the moving truck, driven by Micah from Joanna's team, and then the car with Joanna in it, and then... all hell breaks loose when this SUV comes into view. They pull guns first. See?"

Terry and I watched, and yes, they shot first. Hank's guys barely had time to react, but they got a few shots off before the vehicle took off. Not that it mattered. We may end up charging them as well. That was still to be determined.

"Can you replay it?" I asked.

"You got it." He tapped a few times, and the video started back at the guys coming out the door of Leo's.

We watched it again and then asked him if he could play it in slow motion.

"No license plate." Terry pointed.

"I saw that," I replied.

"We think it's this new group in Redlynne. They haven't really bothered us much since they're kinda far away, and we shouldn't be getting in each other's way, but they have been starting to move around more and more."

"Any idea who the boss is?"

"None. They haven't spoken up or, quote unquote, taken credit for their actions yet. Under the radar type."

"Well, thank you for this information. We appreciate it."

"Sure, I just want to help since they shot my buddy. Al's one of the good ones."

"I agree," Terry said. He then shook Hacker's hand. "We'll let you know if we find anything, and please let us know if you find anything new."

We walked back out and stood in the same spot Hank's guys had been when they were shot at. It was a wonder more of them weren't hurt, just Al. But the guy was huge. It would have been hard for him to duck and get out of the way.

I was also glad that Joanna and her friends had been at the far side of the parking lot when all the shooting happened. She might get under my skin, but I couldn't get her completely out of my heart.

We looked again at the bullet holes and the street.

"This stuff doesn't often happen in Creekview. Maybe you should call over to your uncle," Terry said.

Staring at one of the bullet holes, I realized he was right. I would need to call old Uncle Doug. I hated to do it, but I'd need to know what he knew about them if it was this new group.

"You're right. I'll call him."

We looked once more around before heading back to the station to touch base with our forensic team and write up our reports.

I wasn't looking forward to calling my uncle. He still saw me as a snot-nosed brat of a kid. Perhaps bringing this case to him would finally win me some approval and respect for my position.

Our relationship had been complicated since I was born. The first grandchild, I was spoiled by everyone, especially my grandparents. Uncle Doug was fourteen at the time and hated all the attention I got.

At the time, I didn't understand why he was always so mean. Heck, even thirty-two years later, I still didn't know how he could hate me for just being born.

He'd been the golden boy of the family before my birth. A surprise baby for my grandparents, he'd been the one spoiled until I was born, and then my brother Travis followed me two years later. My grandparents went from active parenting to active grandparenting. How was that my fault?

I didn't think about it again until my shift was over, and I was at home with a beer in hand. It might have been my second.

I drained the beer and then scrolled through my phone contacts. I took a deep breath before pushing my uncle's name.

"This is Hartley." Came his deep voice.

"Hey, Uncle Doug, it's Clint." I choked out. Yes, even at thirty-two years old, my uncle scared me a bit.

"What do you want?" he said gruffly.

"I had questions about an old case. Do you have time?"

"Ha, don't have enough work, ya gotta look in old cases?"

"It's not like that. It relates to a current case."

"Go on."

"I have this friend whose husband died in Redlynne several years ago in a car accident, and she's questioning his death. Then today she was followed, and there was a shooting."

"Um, why do you think this has anything to do with the accident?"

"Because she's been looking into his death and has been being harassed."

"And you think it has something to do with how the case was handled?"

"Yes, it was reported as an accident, but she's saying it was murder."

"So you are suggesting we mishandled the case?"

"No, not at all."

"Who is this person? What's her name?"

I hesitated because if he thought I was crazy before, he would lose it when he heard I was listening to a medium. Well, not so much listening to, but who could argue that she'd somehow solved two cases.

"Joanna Webber," I finally said.

"I don't think I know her. Don't remember a Webber at all."

"His last name was Murphy. She went back to her maiden name after he died."

"Wait, wait, is this that Medium with a Heart?"

"Yeah, that's her. Her husband was in a drunk driving accident about six years ago. Ted Murphy."

"I don't remember that. Six years ago, I'd just moved over here." He paused. "Who is this woman to you? She must be important for you to call me."

"Nobody, just a resident in town. A bit of a celebrity, but that's it."

"I'm not buying it, nephew. Not once in all this time have you called me or asked me for anything. Now all of a sudden, you do?"

"Alright, fine." I was embarrassed to tell this guy that I once looked up to and thought he was the greatest, even if he was mean to me as a child and mostly ignored me my whole life. "We used to date, briefly, but that's it. Nothing serious."

"Uh-huh, I'm not buying that bullshit, but okay, fine. I'll look into it tomorrow and give you a call."

"Thanks, I appreciate it," I said.

"So, how's my loser brother doing?"

"He's good. We're going fishing Saturday out in Appleton."

"Well." He sighed. "Tell him I say hi. I'll call you tomorrow."

With that, he hung up. I stared at my phone a moment. I was typically a confident, assertive person, but this man always reduced me to a blubbering idiot, or at least that's how I felt.

At least I'd made the call. If he came up with anything to prove that the report was correct and this was simply an accident, I could get Joanna to stop putting herself in danger and break her streak. Maybe, just maybe, get her doing something safer with her life. Then maybe, just maybe, we could find our way back to each other.

Chapter Fifteen

~Joanna~

I was finally able to head over to our new office to unpack. It had been a stressful week as I helped Al with his family. Thankfully, he was now out of the hospital. His shoulder would take a while to heal, and he'd have to wear a sling for several weeks, or more likely months, plus nearly a year of physical therapy. But he was alive and back home with his family.

His mother had been nearly inconsolable when I'd talked to her. I talked her through it and got her calm. Then I went every day to ensure they had food and that his mom was taking her various medicines.

Al had told me that his sisters both let her get away without taking them at times, and he always had to stay on top of it using a journal to track everything. It had helped me a lot while I filled in for him.

His sisters were both special needs, so it was understandable that they might not be good at this and needed the extra assistance. They could cook simple meals and clean. One of them had an office job as a receptionist, but the other couldn't work. She was the sweetest lady and helped her mother around the house.

But today, Al was home and could monitor things, and I took the opportunity to get back to my life. I hadn't been to the new office yet and needed to get my stuff unpacked. We'd be seeing clients before long, and I wanted to be settled in when we did.

Micah had already gotten our storeroom in order while Tessa had worked on the reception and waiting areas. She'd sent me pictures, and it looked beautiful. She'd really captured what I'd wanted with a home-like feel. It wasn't too clinical, which I wanted to avoid.

With those two areas complete, I'd just need to work on my private office and the reading room. Once these areas were done, we would be ready for business again. Appointments would start in a few weeks.

I decided to bring Chewy with me again. I liked to have him with me whenever I could, and he liked it too. He'd been extra clingy after the shooting at Leo's, barely letting me out of his sight, so I thought this would help him not be stressed while I was gone.

When I arrived, I saw that both Micah and Tessa were already here working. She was on the computer in the reception area, which was located just to the right of the empty security desk.

I didn't see Micah but assumed he was in the storeroom packing products to be shipped out as we had many online orders to get out.

"Good morning," I said to Tessa as I leaned against the reception desk. "How are things going?"

"Good. I got the last of the appointments scheduled, so now we're fully booked for next month." She confirmed. "And nearly booked for the month after."

"That's great. I hope people are okay with this extended break as we get settled in here."

"So far, most are. A few seemed annoyed, but oh well, too bad. You deserve a break." She smiled.

"You do too." I returned the smile. "I do appreciate all you do."

"My pleasure. Plus, you pay me," she teased.

"Ah, yes. The almighty dollar."

Chewy and I headed back to my private office to have a look. It was full of boxes, but my desk, credenza, and shelves were in place. I'd have to move around the chairs, but that would come as I unpacked boxes and could push them into place.

I let out a sigh, then watched Chewy smell around at each of the boxes. "Where do you think we should start?"

He wagged his tail but kept up his inspection of the new digs.

"I guess the books."

I grabbed the first one, and so it began. They were primarily decorative, but a few were written by other mediums. There were spiritual ones or books written by people interested in the afterlife. I liked to keep up with what others thought, did, or experienced. Plus, I loved books in general.

Next, I unloaded the various knickknacks and placed them on the shelves, my desk, and along the credenza. It was then time to hang my artwork. I just loved the swirling colors of my brightly colored abstract pieces. Lastly, I filled my desk and credenza with my office supplies.

Glancing around, it wasn't quite right, so I pushed the guest chairs in front of my desk, then I moved around a few things on the shelves.

"Better. I should have done this years ago," I said to Chewy. He wagged his tail but didn't move from his sunspot on the floor. "You have a good life, mutt. Maybe your name should have been Riley."

I left him in his spot and went into the hallway to gather the boxes to take out to the dumpster.

That's when I heard an unfamiliar male voice coming from the reception area. His tone was gruff. Probably a client trying to bully Tessa into scheduling a reading before next month. It happened sometimes.

I sighed and peeked through the glass door of my office to where Chewy was lying peacefully on the floor. He'd be fine while I go handle whatever was happening with Tessa and this man.

As I opened the door to the reception area, I realized this was not just a frustrated client. I came nearly face to face with a gun.

I gasped. "What's going on here?"

"Ah, Joanna Webber, finally." The man with the gun said. He was rough-looking. Large, but not Al large. He had a long scar running from his forehead down the left side of his head. Dark, mean eyes, and his black hair was unbrushed and messy.

"Um, I'm sorry. Do I know you?" I tried to say it calmly, but my throat tightened, and my mouth went dry, making it hard to form the words.

"No, but I know you." He gestured with the gun. "My boss would like to speak with you."

I was really regretting not asking Hank to have security here already. I figured we wouldn't need it until I started seeing clients, and who would even know I was here yet?

"Your boss? Who's that?"

"Cecil Edwards."

The world around me spun. I glanced over at Tessa, her eyes wide with surprise and reflecting my own unstable emotions.

"Cecil Edwards?" I asked. "What about?"

"That's not my business to tell. He would like to tell you himself." A menacing grin spread across his face. "Now, please come with me." He waved the gun toward the door.

I didn't want to go with him, but I was too scared not to. He had a scary-looking gun.

I nodded to him. "Tessa, please make sure Chewy gets home and call Janie about the baby."

I could feel panic bubbling inside me at the thought of Oakley. At least she was away from here and safe, but what if I didn't make it back? I couldn't think about that now.

She nodded, keeping her eyes fixed on the gun.

The man glared at her. "And no funny business. She'll be safe, and we'll make sure she gets home in one piece. Unless you do something stupid, like call the cops." He laughed and pushed me roughly out the door.

At his SUV, he pulled out a blindfold, which he secured over my eyes with such force it caused me to yelp, which caused him to laugh. Then he shoved me into the backseat, slamming the door behind me. I fumbled blindly for the door handle but found that it must be child-locked because it wouldn't open.

I heard him open a door and climb in.

"Comfy?" he cackled as he put the car in gear.

With my eyes covered, I couldn't tell which way we went or how long we'd been driving. My mind was going a million miles an hour, wondering what Cecil wanted and if I would ever see my daughter, family, and friends again.

Finally, after about thirty minutes, estimated by the number of songs I counted on the radio, we stopped. That was about how long it would take us to drive to Buckston, where Cecil was headquartered.

I heard the driver's side door open, then shut, and then the one next to me was opened.

"Ready?" he said, laughing as he pulled me out of the car. As much as this guy laughed, I'd secretly nicknamed him the Hyena.

He guided me from the car into a noisy building. I could hear multiple and jumbled voices but couldn't tell if we were in a busy office building, restaurant, or shopping mall. We could literally be anywhere.

After being pulled along with no sense of direction, I heard him knock on a door and a deep voice telling him to enter. The driver guided me into the room, pushed me down into a chair, and then whipped the blindfold off me with his trademark laugh.

Sitting across from me was a meatball of a man. Short, round, with a scarred face and a devil-like smile. Given his reputation, I'd expected Cecil to be a large, monstrous man. Instead, it seemed only his personality was big and evil.

His appearance had me thinking of a fun uncle who told bad jokes and always asked you to pull his finger. But I'd heard the stories and knew he was not that uncle.

"So, this is the famous Medium with a Heart, Joanna Webber," Cecil said, looking me up and down.

"Yes, that's me." I tried to sound cheery and with as much Joanna charm as possible.

"I hear that you've been asking about me."

"Um, no." Hardly at all yet, just the one day and not really since then. I'd been so busy with getting the new office, Al's family, and moving, I hadn't been able to investigate this as much as I'd wanted yet.

"That's not what I've heard," he said, sitting forward.

"Well, okay, I asked a few people, but nothing too serious. Just curious."

"You know what they say about curiosity, don't you, Medium?"

I gulped. "I'm sorry."

"So you're curious about me. What about?"

I took a breath and looked around a little. We were in a windowless office with dark walls and heavy dark furniture. I was stalling but decided I should be honest. I knew there was a chance he would kill me either way.

"My husband was killed several years ago, and as a medium, I recently reconnected with him. He claims he was murdered." I looked at him to judge his reaction, but his face remained emotionless. "He thought maybe it was your guys."

I cringed as I said the last part. However, I wasn't expecting his reaction. He laughed, a big, huge belly laugh.

"Oh, Joanna, Joanna, Joanna, that is the funniest thing I've heard in a long time." He stood and started pacing. Standing, I saw just how short he was. If he was orange, I swear he would be working in a chocolate factory. "I don't even know who your husband is, or I guess was. No Webber."

"His last name was Murphy, but would you remember all your hits? I thought..." I stopped short of saying how many people I thought he'd killed. That seemed tacky and dangerous.

"I remember a lot of them, but no, you're right, I don't remember all of them, especially in the early days. They were just random people in my way to the top."

I shivered at his words. I didn't reply, though, as he continued.

"How long ago was this?"

"About six, almost seven years ago in Redlynne."

"Redlynne, you say. Hmm, yes, I did a few jobs out there back then, but I don't remember a Murphy. How would I have known him? Why would I have ordered a hit on him?"

"He worked for Hank Hammersley."

He chuckled. "Old Hank the Hammer, huh? Yeah, then it's possible I did, but I'm sorry, I don't remember."

I felt my heart sink a little. I didn't know what I'd expected him to say, but it would have been nice to wrap this up and get my closure with one conversation. But given my experience with these things, that wasn't how it worked.

"Is that all you wanted to know, Medium with a Heart?" he asked. The sarcasm on my tagline was obvious.

"Yes, that's very helpful, actually." I started to stand.

"Uh-uh, not so fast. I'm not finished with you yet." His tone was glacier smooth.

I sat down slowly.

"Now, my business." He paused. "I don't want you to speak my name again. Do you understand? Even if I killed your husband, I probably had a good reason."

"Okay, but—"

His hand went up. "No buts. Stay out of my way and out of my business."

"Yes, not a problem." I doubted I would listen, but I couldn't hint that I would continue with my sleuthing as soon as I was out of here. "But may I ask a question?"

"Shoot," he said, one eyebrow raised.

"I need closure on this. Do I just assume you did it and move on?"

He stepped close to me and looked me square in the eye. "That's what I'd recommend."

With that, he snapped his fingers, and the driver put the blindfold back over my eyes, pulled me up, and pushed me out of the door.

Back in the car, he laughed as he drove us away.

Chapter Sixteen

~Joanna~

A few days after my encounter with Cecil, I was still shaking and jumpy from the meeting. Since then, I'd also had several sleepless nights.

However, it solidified my thinking that I was on the right track. The only problem was I didn't know where to go from here.

Hank had warned me to stop, as did Cecil. I knew Clint disapproved, and I'd get a stern lecture from him about putting myself in danger. So what choice did I have but to try not to think about it, at least short term?

However, today I'd made an appointment to take Oakley to see Cate in jail. It had been a while since our last visit, though I'd sent her mail and pictures. Still, she would be surprised by how much her bio-daughter had changed in just a few short months.

I got Oakley dressed in a sweet pink and gold dress I'd bought specifically for today. I knew that Caitlyn had loved the color and picked out the baby's nursery in these colors. She never got to see her use it, except in the pictures I'd shared with her.

"First mommy is going to love this outfit, baby girl," I said as I fixed her hair in two tiny pigtails with tiny little ribbons.

She said something that sounded like mama.

"Yes, we're going to see your first mommy."

"Ma, ma, ma." She giggled.

I got her bag packed and had a few comfort things for Cate on the pre-approved list: magazines, a couple of books, and a few special pictures of Oakley. I'd also add some money to her account so she could buy a few things at the commissary.

Once I had everything together, I loaded the baby into the car, and off we went.

As we drove across town to the jail, I watched the rearview mirror for any car following me. A habit I'd gotten into. Nothing looked out of place, so I thought we were good.

I remembered the last time I'd come to see her. I'd been followed. It had been a scary encounter, but Clint had come to my rescue.

Ten minutes or so later, I parked in front of the jail, got everything unloaded, then headed in to get checked in.

We were escorted into a visitation room to wait for Cate. I got Oakley out of her stroller so I could hand her right over.

The minutes passed with no Caitlyn. I started to get a little worried that we weren't going to get to see her. They'd never taken this long to bring her in.

Finally, the door swung open, and the once bubbly toy poodle came in. Her light, fun personality was muted until she saw her baby.

"Oh, Oakley, baby." She gushed. "She's gotten so big, Jo."

"I know." I said. "How are you?" I stood to hug her.

"I'm okay. Ready for this all to be over." She frowned. "You heard it got delayed again, right?"

"Yeah, I'm sorry. I thought it would be simple for you."

"Me too." She held out her arms for the baby. Oakley looked up at me and then back to Cate. She then squealed and lunged toward Cate. "Oh, baby, do you remember me?"

"I think she does."

I let mom and daughter get reconnected while I watched and stayed quiet. It was strange. I wasn't even jealous. I knew what Cate had done, but I also knew she was remorseful and was paying the ultimate price by not getting to raise her daughter herself.

Not having a family herself, she'd wanted nothing more than to create one, and she had tried. But sadly, her own choices cost her everything, and she knew it.

For me, it was a huge honor to be able to raise this sweet baby.

"So, tell me, what's going on with you? Are you still dating the hot detective?"

"Oh, no. We ended things a few months ago, right before my tour."

"Bummer. What happened?"

"Long story, but I just thought we would be better as friends."

"He didn't look at you like you were just friends."

"Really?"

"Really. He always looked like he couldn't wait to rip all your clothes off." She laughed.

"Ha, Cate, no." Did he? She had to be making that up. "We both held back a large part of ourselves. Both afraid to get hurt again."

"Why? How?" She kept bouncing and playing with the baby while we talked. Oakley poked at and touched her face.

"Well, I can't remember if I told you or not, but my husband died, and I never really got over him. Clint has a similar story. His fiancée was killed in the line of duty."

"Oh, I'm sorry. I do remember you mentioning your husband. Ted, right?"

"Yes. It was just difficult to be in a relationship without closure."

"So what are you going to do about it?"

I hesitated to answer because I honestly wasn't sure if she was asking how I would get closure or how I would just move on.

"Well, I did recently reconnect with Ted, you know, on the other side." I smiled. "He actually told me he was murdered, even though it was reported as an accident."

"Wait. What?"

"Yeah, so I'm looking into it."

"Is there anything I can do to help you? I know, or used to know, a lot of people."

"I'm not sure. The only thing he told me is he thinks it could have been Cecil Edwards. You know who that is?"

"Um, yeah, everyone knows Cecil, right?"

"I just met him recently." I felt my blood turn icy at the thought. He'd been intimidating, and even days later, his tone and glare had me spooked.

"Yeah? Well, I briefly dated one of his guys. They were some of the ones helping me follow you, and Cecil owns that warehouse where I took you. So I knew about it from them."

"How did I not know that?"

"I didn't give them away. I took full responsibility for everything. I mean, it was all my idea. They only did what I paid them to do. Then once I got caught, they went back into the shadows."

I was beyond shocked. I had no idea those were Cecil's men. I only knew she'd hired people to help her. But thinking back, I guess it made sense they would be his as they were from Buckston.

"Can you tell me anything about them?"

"The only thing I would say is to stay off their radar. Cecil hires only the worst of the worst. They don't care who they hurt, and if they think you're in their way, you're done."

"Wow, okay."

"And Ted thinks they killed him? Do you know why he thinks that?"

"Yeah, because he used to work for Hank, though I didn't know that when we were married. I was so dumb and trusting."

"No, I'm sure he could spin a good lie. They all can."

"I'm learning that."

The guard came in, letting us know we had only five minutes left.

"Gosh, these visits are never long enough." She hugged and kissed the baby. "Baby, I love you so much and miss you every single day."

The guard came back. Cate handed Oakley back to me.

"I love you, Jo. Please be safe, and I will hopefully see you both again soon, maybe before I go to prison."

We hugged, and then she was gone. I got Oakley back in her stroller, and then we left.

On the drive back home, I thought about the warnings Caitlyn had given about Cecil. The worst of the worst and hurting anyone they thought was a threat to their business.

I definitely didn't want to get in their way. I just wanted the truth about my late husband. I wanted closure. I wanted peace. Who could blame me for that?

Chapter Seventeen

Yesterday had been a day off as I'd gone to visit Cate in jail. It had been a pleasant visit, and she'd given me some food for thought. Though I still wasn't sure which direction to go with this investigation, I guess I hoped something would just fall into my lap like it had with the other two cases.

Until I could develop a better plan, I decided to head over to our new office. There were always product invoices to review, emails to answer, and checks to sign. That's just what I needed: a full day of work and distraction.

Oakley was with Janie, and Chewy was safe at home. Though I'd thought about bringing him to protect me, I just couldn't put him in harm's way again or stress him out.

I arrived to see both Tessa and Micah were already here. I chuckled a little. When we worked out of my house, I was obviously the first one at work each day. Now the roles had reversed, but at least I wouldn't be here alone.

"This was a good move," I said to myself as I grabbed my purse.

Climbing out of the car, I smiled at the outside of the building. It might be plain beige cement bricks, but the landscaping was nice, with neatly trimmed shrubs and pansies in white, purple, and pink shades.

"Good morning, Jo." Tessa said with a smile as I walked in. "Here are your messages."

"Oh, thanks, and good morning." I took the slips of paper from her. "How are you doing?"

"I'm good."

We hadn't talked much about the run-in with Cecil's gun-toting guy the other day. After getting home that day, I'd called her to let her know I was okay. She brought me Chewy, my purse, and my cell phone. We hugged and made sure the other was alright, but that was the extent of our conversation about it.

She was a woman of few words, but those words were always important.

Nodding at her, I turned toward my office but was stopped by Micah as he came out of the storeroom holding a box.

"Hey, boss."

"Oh, hey. What do you have there?"

"These are those samples of the new products. Just got them. Want to look at them with me?"

"Sure."

I followed him to his office. He set the box down and started pulling out a few items.

"So, this is the new logo?" I asked. "Why do I remember it having more blue in it?"

I reached for my cell phone to check the image he'd sent me.

"No, this is the one." He assured me.

"No, see?" I held up my phone with the image displayed. "It should have more blue in this area."

"Uh, I thought we approved this one." He said, holding the t-shirt up. "I guess I need to check my notes more carefully."

I picked up a mug from the box. The logo wasn't bad. It was three hearts entwined. One was red, one blue, and the last yellow. Then the words Medium with a Heart wrapped around in a mix of those colors. I was expecting it to be an ombre blue font.

"You know what." I paused as I continued studying the design. "Let's keep this one. I do like it better. Not sure why I thought the other."

"Great, boss." Micah sighed. "I'll confirm with the vendor and put in a full order."

"Thanks." I started to walk out.

"Before you go, how are you doing today? Facing Cecil like that."

"I'm okay. I was worried most about Tessa, but she seems fine today."

"Are you going to keep looking into this?" I could see the concern etched in his face.

"I honestly don't know. I feel like the universe is telling me to let this go. Plus, the age of any evidence or clues, there just isn't going to be much, if any."

"Yeah, but it's Ted." He said what my heart was screaming.

"I know." I plopped down into one of his office chairs.

His office was messy, but it was due to his job duties. He was our product guy and handled all the shipping and receiving of our products from vendors and customers.

That meant, even with the dedicated storeroom and packing area, he had boxes, shipping supplies, bubble wrap, and all types of scissors, box openers, and tape dispensers lying around. Maybe I should get him a utility cart to store supplies on, and he could easily roll it around from his office to the storeroom and back.

"I'm willing to help you with investigating this. I know how important this is to you. I remember meeting you just a few months after his death."

I remembered too. I was still crying myself to sleep most nights and was barely eating. All I did was go from one afterlife club or conference to another, looking for answers. I wanted my powers back and to find Ted. Neither happened, at least not until years later, but I gained a friend and my extremely successful business.

"Do you have any ideas? I'm out of places to look or people to talk to." Granted, I still hadn't done a lot of legwork yet, but the trail was so cold it made it hard to find leads.

"Well, do you think Hank has files? Records of his debts, skips, even his employees?"

"I hadn't even thought about that."

I didn't keep many records. Mine was mainly tax forms, invoices, accounts paid, accounts received, and some small things for employing Tessa and Micah. Nothing much at all. This was by design as the nature of my clients, I felt, was private.

Also, in the beginning, I was a fraud, which I hated, but I didn't want anyone finding my research notes on my clients. It would not only hurt my customers, but it could have killed my business if that information leaked out. Thankfully, my powers were back, and I didn't have to fake anymore.

"Maybe we could find out where he keeps them and break in."

"Micah!" I jumped to my feet. "You aren't seriously suggesting we break into Hank's office, are you?"

"I am."

"Oh man, I don't know if that's a good idea at all."

There was a sound at the door. We both looked over. It was Eddie. How long had he been standing there? What was he doing here?

"I can help you with that." He offered. A smile slowly formed on his face. "I was actually coming here to see what else you might need help with and check on you. I heard about Boomer picking you up the other day. He can be scary."

"Boomer? Is that Hyena?" I clasped my hands over my mouth as soon as I said it.

Eddie laughed. "Yeah, that's him. I never heard him called that, but it fits. He's so annoying with that laugh."

"It was annoying." I heard it in my dreams, though I kept that last part to myself. No reason to worry anyone. But that sound was burned into my brain forever.

"Yeah, well, I can get you into the office where the records are kept. It may even give you information on Murph and what skip he was tracking that day."

"Thanks, that would be awesome." Though the thought of sneaking in there, even with one of his trusted employees, had my stomach twisting in knots.

"Great. I'll figure out the best time and send you a text. Maybe lunch later?"

"Sure. I appreciate the help, Eddie." I hugged him without thinking. "Oh, sorry."

"No worries. Always nice to get a hug from a pretty girl." He winked and then turned to leave.

"Oh wait, why don't you have a nickname like some of the others?"

"Who says Eddie is my real name?" He walked out whistling.

When I couldn't hear him any longer, I turned to Micah.

"So, what do you think? Should I trust him?" I felt like I could, but Micah had better instincts when it came to people than I did.

He turned to look out the window, then back to look at me. "I think you can. He seems to care about your safety and, like Al, would probably take a bullet for you."

"Do you want to come along?"

"Probably best I don't, boss. The fewer people involved, the easier it is to sneak in and out without being caught."

"Good point."

We got back to work without further mention of Ted, Hank, or my upcoming break-in. Even if I was going to be led in, it was still sneaking, and if Hank found out, he would probably string us both up.

Chapter Eighteen

~Clint~

I set my gun down after emptying it into the target at the end of my lane. I followed the gun safety steps to ensure the gun was empty and then slid the safety on. I looked to my left to see Terry still firing.

We were at the gun range today practicing. We rarely used our firearms, so getting a few rounds in kept us sharp.

I watched him take a few more shots while I let my mind wander. First to a case I was working on, then to a conversation I'd recently had with my parents about selling their house, and finally it landed on a certain brunette who annoyed the hell out of me. Joanna could get herself into trouble quickly, and I'd heard through the grapevine that Cecil's guy, Boomer, had picked her up recently. Cecil had requested an audience with her. I'm sure it was to warn her to stay away.

No surprise at all. She was too nosy for her own good. If she would just stick with talking to the dead people and their families without getting so wrapped up in the drama of it, she'd be safe.

Terry finished his last shots, and after securing his gun, he turned to me.

"How did ya do?" he asked as he took off his hearing protection.

"Not too bad. Most dead center."

"Yeah? Me too." He smiled. "Felt good to get some stress out."

"Oh yeah, what stress do you have?" I teased.

"Try being married for nearly twenty years with four kids, then you tell me. Oh, and being your partner."

"Touché," I said. "Lunch?"

"Sure. Let's go."

We locked up the practice guns and returned the unused ammo to the armory before heading to lunch.

"Where do you want to go?"

"Quench?" I asked.

"Do you ever go anywhere else?"

"Sometimes, but I never take dates here, so it's usually ex-girlfriend-free."

"Ah, yes." He said. "Speaking of exes, have you talked to Jo lately?"

"No." I didn't want to talk about her either, but I didn't say that out loud. She took up enough real estate in my brain as it was.

"But you heard about Boomer, right?"

"I did."

"You gonna do anything?"

"Honestly, I'd like to stay out of this one, and I've already done more than I wanted by calling old Uncle Doug." He hadn't called me yet, and I wasn't planning to call him again anytime soon. If he hadn't called yet, it meant there was likely nothing to tell. "Plus, Cecil doesn't live in Creekview. We have our own mob boss, and honestly, Cecil didn't do anything wrong."

"Right, but Boomer held her and Tessa at gunpoint in Creekview."

"We don't know that for a fact. It's just a rumor. We can't arrest someone on a rumor." Though I'd love to beat him to a pulp for messing with Jo, I couldn't do that, especially not as a cop.

"I'd love to catch him doing something in our town," Terry said. I saw him tighten his grip on the steering wheel. "Hank at least helps out the town. Cecil does nothing positive."

It was true. Hank was like a nonprofit that helped the homeless and the poor. He also ran a food bank and a shelter. I didn't want to think about how he got his money, but he cared about Creekview and the people living in it.

I didn't ask a lot of questions about how he made his profit, though. It was our unwritten rule with him: stay out of his business, and he tried to stay within the boundaries of the law. Though at times, it was barely legal.

We pulled up at Quench. It was crowded as usual, but the wait was never too long, and the food was worth it. We made our way to the host stand.

"Hey, Clint." The hostess greeted us.

"Hi, Angel. What's the wait?"

"Hmm, ten minutes?" She touched my arm and flashed me a bright smile.

I nodded and stepped out of the way of the next guests in line.

I looked around the packed restaurant but had a limited view of the dining room. Then, after only a few minutes, our name was called by Chris, my favorite waiter.

He walked us to a table, took our drink order, and then went to fill it.

I scanned the familiar menu, knowing I would get my usual.

"I don't come here enough. What's good?" Terry asked.

"I like the burgers, but honestly, almost everything is good." I offered, setting my menu down.

Chris returned with our iced teas.

"So, the usual, Clint?"

"Yes, sir, you know me."

"Great, barbecue burger with extra grilled onions it is, and for you?" He asked Terry.

"Same, but hold the onions. I got my wife to kiss later." He said with a smirk at me.

"Comin' right up."

"Seriously, Walden? Another jab at my relationship status." I said with a chuckle. "I had the best. It's hard to find another like her."

I thought of Monica, and maybe a little bit of Joanna. That's when I heard it: Joanna's laugh. My heart skipped a beat as my eyes started to search for the source of the sound. I found her just a few tables away having lunch with Eddie Cochran.

"What in the world?" I said.

Terry followed my stare. "What do you think they're doing together?"

"I'm sure it has something to do with her husband's death." I couldn't even let myself think they were dating.

"I'm going to go say hi," Terry said, standing and walking over. I sat there frozen with indecision. Should I go?

No, I'd stay here and simmer with jealousy.

I watched as Terry arrived at their table. Jo hopped up to hug him with a smile. That beautiful smile. She then laughed at something he said before she turned to look in my direction. Her smile dulled as our eyes locked. I had tried to look away, but I couldn't.

I offered a weak smile before being saved by Chris bringing our burgers. I peeked without turning my head to see Terry saying goodbye and walking back to our table.

"Oh, this looks good." He said as he slid across from me into the booth again.

"Hmm, yeah," I mumbled as I took another bite. I didn't want to talk, just eat and get out of here.

Thankfully, he ate and didn't offer anything about his brief conversation with Joanna. Our meal ended uneventfully. We paid the bill and walked out at the same time as Joanna and Eddie.

"Hey, Hartley," Eddie said.

"Eddie." I nodded. "Jo."

"Hi, Clint." She said. "How you been?"

"Good." I paused. "How about you?"

"I'm good."

We all stepped outside. She smiled as she and Eddie went the opposite way. As we reached our car, I turned to see her giving Eddie a hug. My blood boiled, and I fought the urge to stop them, but the hug ended as quickly as it started. He opened her car door, then watched her as she drove off.

He then turned and looked in my direction, giving me a nod as he climbed into his truck, all the while smirking.

"Back to work," Terry said, breaking me from my trance.

I stewed all the way back to the station. Terry tried to engage me in conversation, but after several failed attempts, he gave up. He'd known me long enough to understand my moods.

Arriving at my desk, I noticed a voicemail. It was my uncle. I listened to his message asking me to call him back. I dialed his number.

"This is Hartley."

"Hey, Uncle Doug. It's Clint returning your call."

"Hey, kid. Thanks for calling me back." His use of the word kid to refer to me grated my nerves, but I let it go. "I'm glad you tipped me off to the Murphy accident. I think you might be on to something."

"Seriously?" How was Joanna doing this? If this one did pan out, I might have to give this medium thing much more credence. "Whatcha find out?"

"I'd rather we meet to discuss. Can you meet me maybe Tuesday?"

"Sure."

We made plans to meet at a bar halfway between Redlynne and Creekview but away from Buckston, so it would be neutral ground for both of us. It had me wondering why he was so hesitant to talk over the phone, though.

Did that mean Joanna's theory was accurate? Had they been murdered? I'd just have to wait to find out.

At least the phone call had distracted me from thinking about Eddie and Joanna, at least for a moment. Then, of course, later in the quiet of my home with a beer in one hand and the remote in the other, I let my imagination go wild with reasons why those two were having lunch.

There were only two reasons, and neither made me happy. The first, of course, being they were dating. I couldn't even let my mind go there.

The second had to do with her husband's death. I didn't know for sure, but I would guess Eddie had known him. That was the one I was going with because the other had me wanting to punch walls.

"Let it go, idiot," I said to myself and tried to focus my attention on the ball game on the television. "Nothing good will come from opening that door."

When the game got a bit more exciting, I could finally think about something else, and soon it was out of my mind, at least for tonight.

Chapter Nineteen

~Joanna~

It had been a few days since my lunch with Eddie. We'd made plans for the best day and time to search through the files at the office. Though Hank took meetings and conducted a lot of business out of Leo's, he also had a building that he used. He employed roughly two hundred people to run his various enterprises, mainly properties he leased out. He also ran a food bank, homeless shelter, and rehab center.

You wouldn't know by his bad boy, mob boss reputation, but Hank Hammersley does more good for this town than anyone.

My nerves were working overtime just thinking about what I was about to do, even if I was getting help. There was still a risk to both me and Eddie.

Josh and Micah had arrived to babysit Oakley.

"Where's my favorite girl?" Josh gushed as he came in the door.

She giggled at the sight of him, almost jumping from me to him. Once in his arms, she patted his face and babbled away.

"Oh, and then what happened?" Josh said, carrying a chattering Oakley into the living room.

"They're so cute." Micah watched them walk down the short hallway from the foyer to the living room. "I can't wait until we have one or two ourselves."

"Oh yeah? Happening soon?"

"Maybe. I mean, I haven't said anything to him yet, but I'm working on something for our future." He winked. "Is that what you're wearing?"

I looked down at my outfit. I was wearing a black hoodie, black pants, and my only pair of black boots.

"What's wrong with this?"

"Too suspicious. Come on. Let's get you changed."

I followed Micah to my bedroom. He headed straight for the closet and started flipping through my tops.

"Where is that one blue top with the red print?"

"Oh, uh-mm, this one?" I pulled it out.

"Yes, that one, and then your khaki slacks. The ones you'd gotten that stain on that one time."

I'd spilled my spaghetti on myself at a party he had hosted. The stain wouldn't come out for me, but he had worked a miracle and gotten it all out for me.

"Oh, I see what you're thinking." I grabbed them off the hanger. "And my navy pumps?"

"Yes!" he said. "Now change and come show me."

He walked out to the living room, leaving me to change. I stripped off my espionage outfit and put on the more classic outfit he suggested.

After I was dressed, I looked at myself in the mirror. I looked like I was heading for a day in the office rather than a stakeout in a cheesy movie. Micah was always right about my fashion.

"Much better," I mumbled to my reflection.

I stepped into the living room. Both guys were on the floor playing with a giggling Oakley.

Chewy was sitting nearly on top of Micah, who was his favorite person, besides me, of course.

"See, that's better, boss," Micah said. "Now at least you look less suspicious if you did get caught, not like something out of a cliché spy movie."

"Look at the hot mama," Josh teased.

I posed a few times, and we all laughed, including Oakley, though I'm sure she didn't know why.

There was a knock on the door.

"Must be Eddie," I said. "Are y'all good?"

"Yep, we're good. Aren't we, Oakley?" Josh cooed at her.

She said something that might have been a yes.

"Well, good, I'm out." I dropped a quick kiss on her head and sprinted for the door.

"Hey, Jo," Eddie said when I opened the door. "Wow, you look... great."

"Aw, thanks. So do you." Though he actually looked about the same as usual. Tonight's ensemble was a red and gray bowling shirt with dark jeans and brown leather shoes.

"Ready?"

"Yep." Ready to get some information and get this scary-as-hell task behind me.

We drove over, chatting casually and easily. He was a fun, interesting guy. He told me he'd worked for Hank for about ten years, starting as a messenger and working his way up to running security on many of his properties.

"I'm basically the manager of that department. I supervise about fifteen people."

"Considering what I know about the size of the operations, I would think there would be more security than that."

"Oh yes, there are. There are three of us that each manages about the same number of folks. I have the most under me, plus I'm over the other two managers."

"Interesting. Then how is it that you were stuck on surveillance at my house those couple of times?"

"Just part of security. Sometimes the odd jobs fall to my team."

"Ah, okay."

"I love doing security much better than doing the skip tracking. That job sucked. Ted wouldn't have been doing it much longer if he'd bagged that last guy."

"Really?"

"Yeah, he would have likely been doing security or running some of the lease properties."

The security had some potential danger, but the leasing manager's job could have been safer. It would have made starting our family easier and doable. Unfortunately, I'd never know because it never happened.

We arrived at the office building. It looked fairly empty. Though there were a few cars in the parking lot. None looked like the standard-issue mob boss type, so I felt safe enough. Plus, I was walking in with one of the heads of security.

We parked and headed in. He scanned a badge on a wall panel. There was a beep, and the door unlocked.

He opened the door wide. "After you."

"Thank you, sir."

The lobby was spacious, with a beautiful fountain in the middle. To its left was a reception desk. It sat empty at this late hour. Immediately in front of the desk was a fifteen-seat waiting area. The chairs were your standard reception area chairs with a jewel-colored pattern on them.

He walked to the right of the fountain to a double glass door, scanning his card again, and we walked through.

We passed empty offices. I couldn't see in them as their lights were off, but from the little bit I could see, nothing special or crazy in any of them, like dead bodies or piles of cash, which is what my imagination had expected.

It looked like any other office space I'd been in. Nothing screamed out about illegal activity.

"The file room is this way."

I followed him down another hall to a nondescript room with a simple placard on it that read "Records."

He once more scanned his card to gain entrance to the room. We stepped into a dusty, moldy-smelling room with wall-to-wall file cabinets.

"Wow, I'm going to be honest here, I knew you said files, but I thought most people had started to move toward more electronic files."

"Oh, we have those too, but Hank is from a different generation where paper copies were king. We even have a few typewriters in the building, and some of our forms still use carbon."

"Really? That's crazy. I didn't even know you could still buy carbon forms." I looked around the room. "Where do you suggest we start?"

"Here."

He headed toward a cabinet to our left. He opened it and started looking through the names on the folders. He seemed to know what he was looking for, so I just waited.

"Okay, here's what we have on Ted." He pulled out a cardboard folder that was stuffed with yellowing papers.

He handed it to me and gestured for me to sit at a worktable set up nearby. As I sat, he started looking through a different cabinet.

I took a deep breath before opening it. The first item I saw was his face at approximately eighteen years old. I gasped.

Eddie looked over my shoulder. "Oh wow, I almost forgot he started so young."

"I met him about a year after this."

I started flipping through the rest of the papers to see what else was in it and look for anything that could give me leads to follow. It was mainly pay statements and tax forms, but there were some details about jobs he'd done or helped on.

They looked almost like an invoice. I read through a few. It listed the name of the debtor, how much they owed, last known location, how much the enforcer would get for catching them, and then if they were caught.

Goosebumps formed as I found one that listed Redlynne as the location. Checking the date, this had to be it.

"Eddie." My voice shook as I said his name. "I think I found it."

"Let me see." He took it from me. "Now that I see this, I kind of remember this one. I had to go after this guy after he died."

"Oh. Really?"

"Yeah, it felt kinda wrong, but we had to get him or the money."

"So what happened with this guy? Do you think he's someone we should look into more?"

"He's in jail, I think. And, nah, he wasn't the one to kill them. I know that for sure."

I nodded but didn't say anything. I noted his name because I wanted to research him later. I trusted Eddie, but I had to know for myself.

He handed me another file. This one was about the new group running Redlynne. And just like Hank, they mainly did property management. In fact, the more I read, their business was almost a mirror of Hank's.

"This is weird. Do you know much about them? I don't see any names. Just a few nicknames."

"Yeah, nicknames. We really don't know much about them. I've met a few of the goons but no idea who is in charge over there."

"Their business looks so much like Hank's, at least the little I know about it." I read another page, then a thought hit me. "How do y'all have so much information on them, but no names?"

"We try to keep up with any of our rivals. It helps when finding skips and if we have to conduct business in other towns. This one has been harder to nail down because whoever it is really knows how to stay in the shadows."

"I'm seeing dates starting around the year Ted died. Did this group form around that time?"

"I don't remember exactly when, but yeah, it must have." He said, looking over my shoulder again. He dropped a couple of folders on the table in front of me, but before I got a chance to read them, his phone rang.

"Hey, Hacker, what's up?" He said, then listened. "Oh shit. Okay, thanks for the heads-up." He hung up. "We've gotta go, now." The urgency in his tone caused panic to radiate through me.

"What happened?"

"Well, as I told you, Hacker's been playing a loop of this building showing it empty, but Hank is heading over here to conduct some business."

"Ah, got it!" I said. "Let's go."

We scrambled to get the files put away, then walked quickly back down the hall. He looked over his shoulder several times as we exited, and then we nearly sprinted to his truck.

I let out a nervous giggle when we climbed into his truck, to which he winked, sliding the vehicle into drive and heading out of the parking lot.

We'd just gotten down the road and around the corner when we saw a vehicle speed past and turn toward the building.

"I hope he didn't see us," Eddie said, peeking in his rearview.

"Would he chase us?"

"Maybe. Honestly, I don't know. I've never done anything against his wishes before."

"Why are you helping me?"

He looked over at me. "It's you."

I sat there in my shock. What did that mean?

We drove the rest of the way to my house in silence, though a million questions were running through my head. I wished I would have gotten to read more in the files. I wonder if he would agree to take me back another day. I'd keep that in mind if I thought I needed to.

He pulled in front of my house, then turned to me. "Sorry we didn't get to look more."

"That's okay. I didn't really expect to find the answer tonight. Just need ideas of where to search." I said.

"It sounds like Redlynne."

"It does." The thought made my skin crawl. The last time I went, I was followed, and then the threatening phone calls started. What would happen if I went now?

"If you need someone to go with, I'm happy to tag along."

"Oh, um, thanks. I'll let you know." I stammered.

Oh no, why was he helping me so much? Gosh, I hoped he wasn't crushing on me. I don't think I'd led him on in any way.

"Weird question." Oh crap, here it goes. I braced myself for his confession of love. "What was it you thought Ted was doing for his job?"

Wait, what? That wasn't what I was expecting. I tried to keep my face neutral, but I could feel my cheeks warm at my mistake. I was thankful it was dark out, so he couldn't see the blush on my cheeks.

"He told me he was an account manager for a large real estate company, which now thinking about it wasn't a complete lie." I let out a nervous laugh. "Since I really didn't know what that all meant in terms of job duties, I just took what he said at face value. He said he managed properties out of town and attended industry conferences, so I believed it."

"I can see that."

"I really appreciate your help."

"Happy to help." He smiled. "Ted was a good guy, and you're good people, Jo. If Hank has taught me one thing, it's we help others."

"Really?"

"Yeah, I know, I know. He has this bad-ass reputation, but he does all these good things too."

I nodded but didn't reply at first. "I better get in there and relieve the babysitters."

"Well, give me a call if you need anything." He leaned forward, kissing my cheek and then reaching for my door to push it open. "Good night, Joanna. Oh, and remember, this never happened." He winked.

I think I mumbled something as I climbed out of his truck, stumbling a bit as I made my way to my door. I turned as he drove away.

"What just happened?" I whispered as I touched my cheek.

Chapter Twenty

~Joanna~

I was working in my new office, mostly answering emails, which was the bulk of what I did until we started seeing clients again. We got a lot of fan mail, and I liked to answer as many as I could. However, I hated delegating it, so I only asked Tessa in a pinch.

"Knock, knock." Came a familiar, deep voice from the door.

I looked up to see Ted standing there.

"Oh, hey, how've ya been?" I instantly realized what a dumb question it was. He was dead. "Sorry, that's a silly question."

He chuckled. "No, it's a fair question. I'm okay."

"I haven't seen you in a while. I didn't know what to think." Honestly, I thought he'd given up on this idea, even if I hadn't yet.

"Oh, yeah." He looked at me. There was a slight sadness in his eyes. "Sorry about that."

"What've you been up to?"

"Just trying to figure out what to say to you." He sighed. "I was so in love with you, and I was looking forward to creating a family. Then seeing you with your daughter, it hit me in the gut. Well, if I had guts. You know what I mean."

We laughed lightly, then he continued.

"I know it's been almost seven years, but I haven't dealt well with dying. I've met others that seem almost happy. I'm miserable."

"Believe it or not, I've talked to a lot of dead people. What you're feeling is normal. So many wanted more time, have big regrets, miss living. Yes, many have peace and are happy, but there's nothing wrong with how you're feeling."

He smiled. "Thanks, Jo. Seeing you that first day started all the regrets all over again, then going to your home, seeing your daughter, it was a lot, and I needed time to process everything." He shrugged.

"What brings you here today?" I decided to change the subject. If I thought about the part of us that never got to be, I'd be depressed too.

"Ah, yes, so I wanted to see if you've found anything?"

"Some, I guess, but not much."

"So what did you find?"

"Well, Boomer stopped by one day."

"Boomer? As in works for Cecil?"

"That's the one. Personally, I think he should be called Hyena."

His eyes went wide. "Oh shit, Jo! You really did meet him. What happened?"

"He came in here, held Tessa and me at gunpoint, then took me to talk to Cecil."

"Tessa? The goth girl at the front desk?"

"She's not goth. She's just... expressive."

Honestly, she'd been called that before. I loved her style, but not everyone did. It was just Tessa.

"If you say so." He rolled his eyes. "What happened with Cecil?"

"Not much. We talked. He answered some of my questions and then told me never to speak his name again."

"What questions did you have?"

"I asked if he ordered the hit on you. He said it could have been him, but he didn't remember that far back. He also said I should just move on."

He cursed and started pacing. I just sat watching him. He was still so handsome. His dark brown hair was still styled, if you could call it that, much as it was in life. Just long enough to have a slight wave to it. His dark green eyes shone a bit less now, but he was still distractingly handsome.

He caught my stare. His voice came out soft and teasing. "What're you looking at, dumplin'?"

"You know I hate that nickname." I grinned at him.

"I know." He chuckled. "So anything else?"

"I broke into Hank's office the other night. I wanted to look through his files."

"I'm so glad I'm already dead because this would kill me for sure. Why are you putting yourself in such dangerous situations?"

"Because you said you were murdered and asked me to look into it. What was I supposed to do?"

"Well, I guess you have to, but I'm dead, you aren't, and you have that beautiful little girl to think about now."

"So are you asking me to stop looking?"

"No. Yes. Maybe. I don't know." He started pacing again. "I just want you safe, but I also want answers."

"Then I keep working on this."

"Can you just do it safely?" he begged.

"I don't know. That hasn't been my experience in investigating these things."

"Have you done this type of thing before?"

"Oh yeah, twice so far. Both times I got kidnapped. Once I got Oakley out of it, but the second time was the worst. I was held in a cabin for a couple of days before I was able to escape."

He gaped at me. No sound or words came from him. Was his eye twitching? Do ghosts' eyes twitch? Looks like they can. I stifled a laugh, trying to keep a poker face.

A new email popped up, so I looked down for a moment while he got his emotions under control. It was nothing exciting, just standard fan mail. They would mostly say how they loved my show or my book or how the t-shirt was the perfect gift.

Sometimes I'd hear from families I'd done readings for. I loved hearing how the closure I'd offered helped them move on with life.

I looked back at Ted, who had started mumbling to himself. I couldn't understand what he was saying. It was at that moment that I think I found my peace. Whether I solved this or not, I realized I had completely forgiven him, though there was nothing to forgive exactly, but all those years of thinking something else was gone.

I watched him a moment longer.

"I still love you very much. I will likely never stop," I said.

He stopped his ranting and pacing to look at me. His face changing from the angry, confused one to the sweet Ted who brought me flowers or my favorite coffee when he knew I was having a rough day.

"Oh, Jo, I feel the same. I hate that our story ended the way it did."

We didn't say a word for several minutes as we both soaked in the sweet moment between us.

He broke the silence first this time. "What's your next step in this?"

"Honestly, I don't know, but I think I need to go back out to Redlynne. I'm just not looking forward to it."

"My parents are out there now."

"Really? I hadn't realized that." I hadn't found that in my internet searches, but I also didn't pay that much attention to information about them, just Ted. "I did see them recently, here in Creekview."

"Oh? How'd that go?"

"You know how your mom just loves me." I rolled my eyes.

"I'm sorry. I wish I was still alive to be a buffer like I was before."

"She'd probably be less upset with me if you were still around too."

"Maybe." He said. "Well, I better get going for now. I'll try not to wait so long to visit again."

"I hope so."

He flashed a smile and then left. I sat there staring at the spot. I felt at peace and had closure, but with the forgiveness came new feelings of grief.

I liked my life now, but I really did miss that type of relationship. A lover that you had special moments with, like when you pass them and give a touch on the arm or shoulder, a sweet kiss when the mood strikes.

Maybe with this bit of forgiveness out of the way, I could finally let myself find that someone again. I wanted it not just for myself but now for Oakley. Sure, a single parent could raise a child to be successful, confident, and well-rounded, so if it didn't happen, we'd be fine.

I let out a sigh and then got back to work. Well, actually, I decided to do some research on Ted's murder.

After the sort-of break-in with Eddie, I couldn't get that skip's name out of my mind. Eddie had said the guy was in jail and wasn't a suspect, but I couldn't help but wonder about him.

I pulled up his name on my computer. Frank Nelson. There were several.

"Ugh, which one?"

I clicked a few to see what it said. Not this one. Not this one. After a few more, I was feeling discouraged.

Then a news article caught my eye. It was an arrest in Redlynne.

"This has got to be the right guy."

I read through it. He was picked up for selling drugs and was currently in prison. I sighed. Eddie had been right about that part.

I guess that was a dead end.

I let my head fall to my desk, not sure what to do from here. This person didn't seem to be the threat, but someone had been. I had to figure out who.

Even if I was starting to forgive him, and he seemed to be finding some peace, I couldn't let this nagging feeling go. I had to know the truth about his death.

Chapter Twenty-One

~Clint~

I pulled up to the bar about ten minutes early. Even though I didn't know what vehicle my uncle drove these days, I still glanced around the parking lot. There were a few trucks, a beat-up sedan, and a couple of motorcycles. Nothing stood out as Uncle Doug's, not that I expected a sign on it saying Uncle Doug's vehicle, but it was worth a look.

Stepping in, I surveyed the room. No Uncle Doug. I made my way to a booth in a corner and sat so I could see the door. A waitress asked for my drink order, and then I waited.

While I waited for my beer, I took in the room. It was a typical bar. Booths around the outside with high-top tables with stools scattered inside. There was a side room that I could only see a bit of, but from what I could see, it was the game room with pool tables and dartboards.

If I wasn't here for business, I would have gone in there and shot a game or two. Add in a few beers, and it would be a great afternoon. But instead, I would be talking about an old case that I wasn't even sure was worth my time and with the one person I wanted to see the least.

The waitress brought my beer.

"What else can I get ya, honey?"

"I'm waiting for someone. Maybe once he arrives?"

"Sure thing." She winked and sashayed away. I watched her go. Not my type, I thought.

Within minutes of receiving my beer, in strolled my larger-than-life uncle. The person who had been both my hero and tormentor of my childhood.

I hadn't seen him in at least ten years. He'd gotten old. His once jet-black hair was now more salt than pepper. It was cut short, close to his head. He still was quite fit, though his middle had gotten a bit rounder. His face showed some age with laugh lines around his eyes, but overall, he still looked like Doug.

We locked eyes as he spotted me. He sauntered over and slid across from me in the booth.

"Hey, kiddo."

"Hey."

He flagged down the waitress, ordering himself a beer. Then he asked me, "Want something to eat? They have great burgers. My treat."

"Sure."

When the waitress returned with his beer, we ordered food. He flirted with her, causing her to blush. He'd always been a bit of a ladies' man. With a giggle, she scurried off to place our order.

"Alrighty, now to business." He gave the bar a once-over and lowered his voice. "I did some digging, and your lady friend might be on to something."

"Yeah?" I sat forward, leaning onto the table.

"Yeah. The chief at the time was doing some corrupt things. Signing off on false reports, he had several officers doing improper investigations, covering up illegal activity, and working with some gang. From what I can tell, this group paid the officers nearly double their salaries."

"If I remember correctly, they all got fired and incarcerated."

"Yep, that's how I got brought in as chief. Most of the department is new." He took a long sip of beer. "Anyway, so I looked at the reports from this accident, and it doesn't sound right."

"In what ways?"

"They didn't check security feeds from the area. Only took a couple of witness statements, but the named witnesses are now in prison as well. They were picked up a few months before everything fell apart with the department."

"What charges?"

"Aggravated assault and burglary. But my guess is they were working with this new Redlynne gang."

"I've heard a bit here and there about them. Any idea who's in charge?"

"No, we've been trying to figure that out. They're under the radar. Way under, though the last few years, they've been gaining more and more traction."

"What do you know about Cecil Edwards? Does he do anything around Redlynne? Or even Hank Hammersley?"

"Both actually do some work out there. Mostly Cecil, not as much Hank."

"Hmm, okay."

"Why? What're you thinking?"

"She works closely with Hank."

"She, your lady friend?"

I fought the urge to roll my eyes. "Yes, her. Joanna."

"Oh right, that medium. Go on." His sarcasm was not lost on me.

"She's worked with Hank a few times now and has become friends with a few of his guys. There was a shooting recently that involved an unknown group and Hank's team. She was followed by this unknown group, and she ended up at Leo's, where Hank hangs out."

"Hm, interesting. Then why'd you ask about Cecil? Something happen there?" Doug asked.

"Well, she was also picked up recently by Boomer, you know, Cecil's guy?" He nodded. I continued. "He drove her to Cecil. That's all I know so far about that."

"You think either of them is involved in this accident?"

"It could be, but I honestly don't know. I was hoping you had more information on the accident."

"Unfortunately, what I have is tainted and not really conclusive. I have a team reviewing what we do have: pictures, the tox report, and the autopsies."

"There were autopsies done for a car accident? I mean, I guess if they were trying to determine drugs and alcohol in their systems, but from what I'd read, their deaths were caused by the accident."

"Yeah, exactly how it was written up. It shouldn't have been necessary, but like you said, not unheard of." He took a sip of beer. "I'll let you know what my team finds out."

"I'd love to come out and review the evidence and reports if you'd allow it."

He stared at me. I could almost see his gears turning as he tried to decide if he'd let me.

"Fine. Sure. Just give my team a little more time to review, and I'll call you."

"Sounds good."

With business out of the way, we got caught up on family news. A cousin getting married, an aunt and uncle getting divorced, holidays, and our missed grandparents, his parents.

The food arrived, and as he'd said, it was a good burger. Not quite as good as the ones at Quench, but a solid hamburger.

After the food was eaten and while we waited for the check, a thought struck me.

"How long were the witnesses sentenced to?"

"I think they got ten years."

"Any chance of early release?"

"Why? What're you thinking?"

"Well, I'm wondering if they could be released soon."

"Uh, maybe, but I doubt there's a threat there."

"If they worked for this new group, they may go back to them when they're released. Could be a lead there if we keep an eye on them."

He stared at me for a moment. His gray eyes burning a hole in my head. I shifted under the weight of his gaze. I had images of him as a young adult, staring at me much like that, right before he pushed me down or laughed at me for some dumb thing I said.

"You might have a point there."

I was slightly stunned that he agreed with my thinking. I was sure he would argue with me.

"Yeah, they'd have trouble getting other work, so it makes the most sense," I added.

"I'll have one of my folks check into that too. See exactly if and when they're going to be released."

"Well, let me know if I can do anything from Creekview."

He laughed. "I'll keep that in mind."

With lunch wrapped up, we headed outside.

"I'll call you when my team has finished reviewing things and let you know what they find." He turned toward a dark gray truck. Now I knew what he drove.

"Thanks for the info and for lunch."

"My pleasure. Good luck with the lady friend. Your mom will be thrilled when you're finally married."

"She's just a friend." Saying it out loud made me feel childish. "Mom knows about her, though."

"I'm sure. Well, take care." He climbed into his truck and left.

I stood there watching him go. That was an interesting conversation. We'd actually spoken like colleagues for once, for at least part of the conversation anyway.

To hear that Joanna's theory could have legs also caused me to pause. I might have to start believing in this medium business if she kept this up.

Chapter Twenty-Two

~Joanna~

"Thanks for watching her today," I said to Tessa as I prepared to head out to Redlynne for the day.

"Of course, I'm happy to," Tessa said. "Plus, it's my turn to have this little cutie."

She laughed and carried the baby into her house. I knew Ms. Ruby would be thrilled to find her here when she got home from the store. She doted on Oakley as if she was her own grandchild.

I smiled and walked to my car for the long ride out of town.

After my talk with Ted a few days ago, I'd decided another trip out there might be in order. Just like my last time out here, I had no good plan. I was just going to drive around and see what happens.

But first, I planned to stop by his gravesite again since Buckston was on the way. I felt this draw to go there. Maybe it was hope I would see him again.

I smiled at the thought. He looked like the same Ted I'd been so in love with. All the anger and hate were replaced with those same old feelings of love and appreciation. All that love I had felt for him was coming back and confusing me at the same time.

I had to remind myself that he was dead, and this was not a relationship I could pursue. Peace and closure felt good, though. Perhaps it would finally allow me to open up to someone else, especially if that someone could get past my job, which had also been a problem in my past relationships.

I thought about Clint. I hadn't quite let myself fall completely for him. Close, but to protect myself, I'd held back. It wasn't fair to him, and I knew he wasn't ready. It was best to just be friends.

This was a talk I had with myself at least once a week, trying to convince myself that I'd done the right thing. When I ended things, he didn't react much, which I think hurt almost as much as ending things. And now, he just seemed like that same angry, arrogant version of Clint that he was when I first met him.

"Ugh, don't think about it, Jo," I told myself.

I turned the radio on a little louder to drown out the thoughts in my head. I sang along with it all the way to the cemetery.

I pulled in and drove around to where his headstone was. I sat in the car, looking at it in the distance. I couldn't see him from here, so I got out and walked slowly, being careful not to step on any of the other graves.

When I reached it, I read the words on the stone, just like that first day I was out here. I chuckled, looking around in hopes of seeing him. My heart sank a little when I didn't.

I turned to leave when a car pulled up behind mine. It was just a nondescript silver sedan, so I didn't think much of it until the driver got out. I froze.

"Well, Joanna Webber, the Medium with a Heart." Cecil chuckled and made his way toward me. The last time I met him, I was seated, and he was standing. I knew he was short, but I was easily three inches taller. At only five foot five inches myself, I wasn't tall.

"Um, oh hi."

"You seem surprised to see me."

"Well, of course. I wasn't expecting anyone else to be out here."

"Yes, well, after I talked to you, I thought about your husband. I thought about all the hits I made." His words made me want to run, but I stood firm. "I think I do remember him, but I didn't order a hit on him, nor was I the one to kill him."

While I stood there struggling with my fight or flight instinct, he'd piqued my curiosity enough to be interested. My nerves calmed slightly.

"Is this him?" He pulled out a picture. It was Ted.

"Yes, yes, that's Ted." I looked from the picture to Cecil. "How do you have that?"

"Because he worked for me six years ago."

"Wait, what? No, no, he said he worked for Hank."

"Yeah, he did, but I was trying to get him to leave and come work for me, so he was doing some smaller jobs for me."

"That doesn't make sense."

"Why not?"

"Because he only told me about Hank. Why would he keep lying to me?"

"I can't answer about the lies, but as far as I know, he never told Hank or anyone."

I stared at this round little man who had just revealed to me yet another secret that my dear, old hubby failed to mention. Ted had told me he thought Cecil had him murdered. Was this the reason for it? I was having a tough time wrapping my head around this.

"So wait, you didn't order a hit on him, right? You were trying to recruit him."

"That's right." He glanced around me at the headstone. "He was the best at collecting and moving cash."

"Moving cash?"

He laughed. "Money laundering, Medium. He knew how to funnel it through casinos, through legit businesses, hiding it in plain sight to make it look clean. He could make a dollar into five or ten or thousands."

"I don't understand. How...?" I had no words. Everything I'd felt for Ted was back in the blender. This man was complex. Would I ever get closure and peace? Would I ever get the whole truth about his life?

"I'm sorry to be the one to shatter your image of him. That wasn't my intention. I just wanted to set the record straight for myself. I didn't kill him. Unfortunately, there is still someone out there who did." He laughed. "Not that I care if people think I did, but sometimes I have a conscience, and I could tell how important this was to you."

A lump was in the back of my throat, and my stomach churned. More lies. More lies from Ted.

"Do you know anything about the new group in Redlynne?"

"The Red gang? Nah, not much about anyone. They've gotten in my way a few times. Buying the property I was looking at. They're trying to copy what Hank does. Heck, I've been doing that as well. He has a great model to follow. All his business looks clean and on the up and up, but he's dirtier than an old pig." He stared at me. "Don't trust him. He'll smile to your face while he's stabbing you in the back and cleaning out your bank account."

What? That hadn't been my impression of Hank at all. We'd worked together a lot, and he always seemed so honest with me. I didn't know Cecil at all, only just having met him. He could be the one lying to me.

I just nodded my head as I tried to process everything.

"Well, Joanna, I will leave you now. Sorry to intrude on your moment here." He gestured to the headstone. Then he turned toward his car, giving one last look at me before driving off.

I turned slowly to look at Ted's name on the marker and then let the tears fall.

"You son of a bitch. You lying bastard." I fell to the ground, hitting it with my fists a few times.

I cried and cried until I had nothing left to give. Then, for good measure, I flipped off his headstone before getting back in my car to drive home. Screw Redlynne and the Red gang. Screw Hank. Screw Cecil, but most of all, screw Ted.

On the drive home, I fluctuated between screaming mad and yelling through tears. It was ugly, and I didn't even care what people in the other cars thought. It wasn't like I would see them again.

I did, however, care what Tessa and her family thought, so before I drove over there to pick up Oakley, I stopped at my house to wash my face and calm down a bit.

"Why?" I yelled at my reflection in the mirror. "I just want the whole truth. Why is that so hard?"

Chewy licked my hand that was clutching the edge of the counter. When I looked down, his big doggy smile and the simple wag of his tail melted my heart.

"Oh, Chewy, you're the best boy." I sank to the ground, and he climbed into my lap for cuddles. He let me cry on him.

I wallowed in my sorrow for far too long, but when I was finally cried out, I praised my dog, rewashed my face, and went to get my daughter.

I steeled myself for the line of questions I knew was coming from Tessa about why I was back so soon. I just hoped I'd be able to tell her without breaking down again. I didn't want to waste any more tears on Ted.

"You're back early," Tessa said when she opened the door. "What happened?"

Immediately, tears started anew, so much for my pep talk on the way over. She put her arms around me, and from somewhere Ms. Ruby came, wrapping her arms around me in a warm embrace when she reached me.

"He lied. He lied more... or maybe Cecil lied." I sniffled, trying to calm myself.

"Come. Tell us all about it." Ms. Ruby said, guiding me to their den where I saw Elsa playing with Oakley. Their house always smelled the best, like home-cooked meals, laughs, and love.

When Oakley saw me, she squealed and crawled to me, pulling up on me. I scooped her up.

"You missed me?" I asked, kissing her cheek.

She grabbed my face and slobbered all over my cheek. I took that to mean yes.

Tessa brought me some tea as I filled them in on my conversation with Cecil.

"Do you believe him?" Tessa asked.

"I don't know what to believe anymore. It sounds believable, and what does Cecil really have to gain from telling me?"

"That's true," she agreed.

"So what now?" Ms. Ruby asked. "Where do you go from here?"

"I honestly don't know."

They insisted we stay for dinner, arguing that I shouldn't be alone right now.

"Plus, we haven't gotten enough time with Oakley," Elsa added.

"Fine, fine," I said, laughing.

Hours later, with a full belly, a container full of leftovers, and a fuller heart, I loaded up my daughter, and we headed home. I was thankful for good friends who were more like family. I tried hard not to think about Ted and Cecil and any of it.

I should never have started this in the first place. Maybe my mom was right. I should look for a regular job and stop with this talking to the dead nonsense.

Chapter Twenty-Three

~Joanna~

Now that we were settled into our new office, it was time to look for a new house. I hated the thought of it. This was the perfect location, the perfect fit, but the safety of myself, my daughter, and my dog were more important. What's the saying? Home is what you make it, or home is where the heart is, or maybe home is where you hang your hat.

I had a lot of phrases to draw strength from. I simply had to pick one and try focusing on it. It might help me with this next big change in my life. I hated change.

I tried not to think of Ted and his lies or what Cecil had told me. Unfortunately, I had no actual proof, and I had to just keep living my life.

Janie had Oakley for me while I went to meet the real estate agent. Even though LaDonna hadn't been able to find us an office space that worked, I decided to give her a chance to help me find a house.

I'd agreed to meet at her office, and we'd head out to look at places from there.

As I'd gotten into the habit of when I drove around now, I watched for any sign that a car was following me. It was even more critical now that I would be moving. I didn't want anyone to know where I'd moved.

Thankfully, it didn't appear like it, though there were a few moments I wasn't sure. I said a silent apology to those innocent souls I thought were following me.

Pulling up, I found a visitor parking spot and then headed in.

"Hello, welcome to Creekview Realty. How can I help you?" The receptionist greeted with a smile.

"Hi, I'm Joanna. I'm here to meet LaDonna."

She tapped on her keyboard. "Oh, yes, Joanna Webber, right?"

"That's right."

"I'll let her know. Just give me a moment." She gestured for me to have a seat.

I only had to wait a couple of minutes before LaDonna came to greet me.

"Hey, Joanna. Come on back."

She guided me into an open area with a large conference table in the center. Around this were offices. The offices had a glass wall separating them from the main room and each of the other offices.

We made our way into the far corner office. It was decorated with personal pictures and a few plants. Most of her office supplies and desk accessories were purple, so I guess she liked purple. I was fond of yellow. I smiled at her as I sat.

"So, I have a few that I thought might fit for you and Oakley."

"Oh, great."

She passed me a few printouts. I flipped through them quickly.

"Are we looking at all these today?" There were about six. I wasn't sure if we could see them all in one day.

"I have appointments set with these three." She pulled out three. "Then these two are empty, so depending on timing, we can swing by to see them. This last one is represented by us here, so it will be easy to get an appointment today if we need it."

"Okay." Sounded easy.

"Did I get close to what you were looking for with these?"

I'd told her a minimum of three bedrooms, two bathrooms, a two-car garage with a large backyard. A porch was a plus, as was a neighborhood with a park or two. I wanted to be within fifteen minutes of my office and my sister.

"Yes, these all look right." Skimming through the pages again, they looked promising, but a lot of things looked good on paper. Unfortunately, those things often turned out to be too good to be true, like Ted.

"Great, the first appointment is in twenty minutes, so we should start heading that way."

I brought the one-sheets with me, and we made our way to her car. We made small talk on the way over to the first house. She asked me about medium work and how the new office was working out for me.

"It's nice so far, though we haven't had clients yet. We'll start seeing them tomorrow."

"Oh, great. I'm sorry I couldn't find you the right fit, but Hank does own some great properties."

"Have you worked with him before?"

"I've sold him some properties, and he's sold some through us."

"Do you know how long he's done property management?"

She shifted a bit in her seat. "Um, I don't... I'm not sure. A long time."

She looked over, giving a tight smile.

"Does that mean you know about his business?"

"Yes," she whispered.

That's odd. We were the only two in the car. Who would hear us? I let the subject drop as we pulled into the neighborhood.

"Alright, so you'll see here near the entrance, there's a nice park with a playground, pond, a community pool."

It was a newer subdivision, and while nice, it wasn't as quaint and charming as my neighborhood park, but Oakley would have fun on the slides, climbing structures, and swings, especially once she was a bit older.

I also noted the trees here were much younger, not as much shade. Of course, there were sidewalks for walking, but our walks would be hot without the shaded trees.

We finally pulled up at the cookie-cutter house that looked as much like the neighbor's house as it did the other neighbor's house. Only the brick color made them look different. Same landscaping, same front elevation. No charm or character, like I had in my current home.

We parked as she reminded me of the details and price of the house. Then we walked through, and while it was neat and clean, nothing stood out to me, and I forgot all the features as soon as we walked out.

There was nothing wrong with this type of house, but I loved my cute place, and that's why I likely saw the negative. Though perhaps this would offer me a bit of anonymity. I'd definitely consider it for that reason.

We made our way to the next, which was basically a different color of the same house. But again, nothing screamed that this is my new home.

The third house was in a different subdivision. It was closer to my sister but in an older neighborhood, which I liked. The trees were mature, the homes had character with porches and gingerbread trim. No two houses looked exactly alike.

The park was full of old oaks and pines with playground equipment dappled in sunlight right in the middle. This reminded me a lot of my current neighborhood.

We pulled up at a lovely craftsman-style house. The picture on the flyer did not do it justice.

A few steps led up to a navy blue door and a wide, covered porch. The house was painted a blueish gray trimmed in bright white.

I smiled. This was perfect, at least from the outside.

"This couple is relocating and have already started to pack. They've asked that we ignore the half-packed-up state of the house." She said with a chuckle.

Stepping in, I noted beautiful wide plank hardwood floors, arched doorways, and a stacked stone fireplace. I barely noticed the boxes.

I could picture my living room furniture in here. Oakley playing on the floor with Chewy, sleeping in the sunbeams coming in from the front windows.

The kitchen was in the back, with large windows overlooking the gorgeous backyard. I stood at the sink, looking out over the backyard. I could picture myself here washing dishes or cooking while the baby, now in my mind a young child, running with the dog in the yard. I'd dry my hands and join in their game of chase.

The bedrooms were all on the same side of the house. A slight change from my current home with its split floor plan. I liked the idea of being on the same side of the house as Oakley, though.

The two secondary bedrooms shared a bathroom, while the main bedroom had its own. As I stood in what I imagined would be Oakley's room, it would be painted pale pink and have gold accents, just the way her bio-mom would have wanted it. I could see a rocking chair or glider in the corner near the window. We'd sit together to read each night.

I felt at home and knew this was where we belonged.

I turned to LaDonna. "It's perfect."

"Really? Oh, great!"

"Yes, I love it."

"Let's head back to my office, and we can put in an offer."

We arrived at her office. She worked up the offer and extended it to the representing realtor.

"It may take a day or two for them to get back, but I know this couple is very motivated to get this sold."

"I am motivated to get moved as well."

We'd already started the paperwork on my house but hadn't officially put it on the market. I wanted to wait until we found a place. There was no rush at all. However, now that we'd found the one, I was ready.

"I wouldn't worry too much. The market is hot right now, and your house will sell as soon as we list it."

"That's great. I'm so ready for this change."

"I'll be over tomorrow to put up the sign, and we can get started."

On the way to Janie's to pick up Oakley, I sang along with the radio. The relief I felt at having found a new home. A place that I could really picture us in, and it could feel like home.

I was also looking forward to seeing clients tomorrow. While I hated my own recent connection with the other side, I did miss reconnecting families and friends with their loved ones on the other side. It was the best feeling to see love, hear their memories, and see the tears of joy.

Once I had Oakley, I talked to her all about the new place we would live. She babbled in reply to everything I said. I doubt she understood and was simply happy to see me and was feeding off my excitement, but I still liked our little conversation and pretending she understood me.

"And we'll paint your new room the same pink it is now. We'll take all of your toys."

"Dawg... dawg."

"Yes, and we'll take Chewy with us."

"Dawg." I could hear her clap. She loved him.

We pulled up the driveway to find the words "Watch yourself bitch" spray-painted on my garage.

I didn't know if I should laugh or cry. Laugh at the irony of finding a new place just today or cry because who the heck had done this, and why hadn't my alarm system picked them up?

I placed the oh-too-familiar call to the police department and then waited.

Chapter Twenty-Four

~Joanna~

The next day, LaDonna called to tell me my offer had been accepted on the house. That was fast with no negotiation at all. I was thrilled. I'd made a competitive offer, though, so it shouldn't have been much of a surprise.

"They're hoping you can close on the house in a few weeks."

"I'd love to, but of course, it will also depend on my house." I wanted out of this house as soon as humanly possible but didn't tell her that.

"Great," she said. "And I'll be over in a few hours to put the for sale sign out. I think I already have some interest in it."

"Really? It's not even officially for sale yet."

"I told you. Things aren't staying on the market long."

I was excited to have this chapter of my life behind me, or at least soon it would be, and on to the next, hopefully safer part of my life.

"Well, like I said, I'll be over later to put out the sign and then get this bad boy sold for you."

"Thanks, LaDonna."

Thankfully, I was able to get my garage cleaned and repainted last night, so it would just be a bad memory for me, and a potential buyer would be none the wiser. Unless they watched the news or any of my neighbors spilled the beans about it.

Stan checked my security camera, and there wasn't anything wrong with it, but somehow the garage artist had been able to avoid it. The cops took a report, but they said they couldn't do much else for me without witnesses or a video. Of course, I already knew this, but I also wanted the vandalism on record, just in case.

I tried not to think about it as I headed over to the office for my first day seeing clients. Instead, I was looking forward to my full day of readings to keep my mind busy.

Pulling in, I saw a few extra cars in the parking lot besides Micah's and Tessa's, because, of course, they were here before me. One should be a security guard provided by Hank. Unfortunately, I didn't know who the others belonged to. I had to assume clients here for a reading, though that would put them here nearly thirty minutes early.

No matter, I hopped out, excited, and headed in.

"Joanna!" I was greeted by a large group.

Tessa looked up with a smile. "These are the McCartneys. Your first appointment of the day."

They were browsing through the small display of books and various tchotchkes we'd set up in the reception area. It was like a mini gift shop full of all the Medium with a Heart must-haves. I'd really been on the fence about setting it up. It seemed tacky, but my team talked me into it, and by the looks on those browsing it now, it was a good idea.

"Oh, great. Hi McCartneys." I smiled. "Let me get settled in the back, and then we'll be ready. Tessa, can you join me?"

I nodded to the security guard. He replied with a nod as well. I'd have to officially meet him later.

Once in my office, I turned to Tessa.

"What time is the appointment?"

"Nine."

I checked the time. It was only 8:30.

"That's what I thought. They're very early."

"They've been here since eight."

"I guess I'm not the only one excited. Any messages?" I asked as I stowed my purse in my desk.

"Not yet." She handed me a printout of my schedule. "I'll let you settle in. Just let me know when you're ready for them."

"Thanks."

I fired up my computer and did a quick scan of my emails. Nothing that couldn't wait. I then ran to see Micah first, and then I would swing by the kitchen for a cup of coffee for myself and some bottles of water for the family.

"Hey, boss."

"Hey, how's it going today?"

"Not bad, not bad." He grinned. "I see you have an enthusiastic group waiting."

"It looks that way." I laughed. "Anything you need from me before I get started?"

"Not a thing, boss. Have fun!"

I headed to our breakroom, fixing myself a mug full of hot coffee with a hint of sweetener and a splash of creamer. Then I loaded up a wicker basket with water bottles. I carried these back to our reading room, placing the basket on the coffee table in the middle. Lastly, I ensured there were plenty of tissue boxes. I gulped down the coffee, burning my tongue a bit in the process, then I ran back to my office for one last check of my email before letting Tessa know I was ready.

The McCartneys came in full of energy, which just stoked my excitement.

"Welcome, welcome. Have a seat anywhere."

"Thank you. We're so happy to see you today." The oldest lady said. "I'm Martha. This is my daughter Jenn, son-in-law Johnny, their children Aiden and Marley. Then my sister Betsy and her children, Tim and Steven."

"Nice to meet you all." I smiled. "Please help yourself to a bottle of water. There are tissues, just in case."

A few of them grabbed a bottle. The ladies all grabbed a few tissues.

"Okay, so how this works is I'll try to connect with your loved one or loved ones. I'll speak mostly as they tell me, so what they say, I'll say for them. Not a lot of he said or she wanted me to tell you. Any questions?"

They all shook their heads.

"There are two people here at the moment for you. Both men."

The first man spoke. "I'm her husband." He gestured to Martha. "I'm Chester."

"I have Chester here."

Martha gasped and immediately started patting her eyes with a tissue.

"Chester? Oh, my Chester."

"Hi, Martha, baby. I'm here," I said for him.

"I'm so glad you're here."

"I'm here too," said the second man. "I'm Betsy's husband, Luther."

I introduced him, and Betsy started crying. As the reading began, the whole family was in some degree of tears with laughs mixed in.

They shared stories and memories. There were lots of laughs and inside jokes. I could tell this family had loud holidays and other get-togethers. I loved it. It was just the recharge I needed after all the recent stress.

"Well, we're coming to the end of our session. Any final words?"

"I will be close by you all for as long as I can. I love being able to just watch you all continue to live," Chester said.

"Me too. I'll be here. I miss you so much, my Betsy Lou and my boys," Luther added.

With those final words, I walked them out to Tessa and then introduced myself to the security guard.

"Hi, I'm Joanna."

"Of course. I'm Catfish... err, um, Percy."

"Catfish? I'm sure there's a story there."

He shifted and flashed me a sheepish smile. "It's not a story for a lady."

"Well, Percy then. Thanks for being here."

"It's my pleasure to guard the one and only Medium with a Heart. I'm a huge fan."

"Oh, thank you." I smiled and then turned to watch the McCartneys leave. With their departure, I finally had a break.

I first went into the reading room to clean it and get it staged for the next clients, minus the water, which I'd bring in right before the reading.

I then headed to my office so I could answer some emails. I noticed a couple of missed calls on my cell phone. One was LaDonna saying she had an offer on my house. Then a second from her with yet another offer. The third caused my blood to run cold.

"I hope my warning was enough to keep you out of my business and out of Redlynne."

I stared at my phone. It was one sentence, but the tone was unmistakable. How had they gotten my cell phone number? It wasn't published anywhere. I didn't recognize the gritty male voice at all.

I needed to report this, but I didn't have time right now as Tessa announced my next appointment was here. So I ran to the bathroom quickly and to the kitchen for more bottles of water.

The reading wasn't as lovey as most. The couple had been in the middle of a bitter divorce. Despite that, they had some good memories to share with each other. You could tell they'd had love between them, which is why she'd made the appointment.

After the appointment, I called the police to report the call. Unfortunately, once again, they could only take down the details but not do anything.

"Great. I'll be dead before they decide to do something," I mumbled.

I laid my head on my desk. This was exhausting. I was barely even investigating it this time, but I guess I'd done enough asking around to get attention.

"You okay, boss?"

I jumped up. "Micah, you startled me."

"I'm sorry, but I was walking by and saw your head down."

"I'm okay. Just got a threatening voicemail." I picked up my phone and navigated to my voicemail to play it for him.

The menacing voice gave the short threat again.

"Did you report this?"

"I just did."

"Good. What did they say?"

"Not much, just like any other time. They can only take a report of what happened."

"Now I see why your head was down. Frustrating."

"Yeah." I exhaled. "In other news, LaDonna has two offers on my house."

"Well, that's great news! Did you accept one?"

"Not yet. I still need to call her back."

"What are you waiting on?"

I didn't have time to call her back as my third appointment of the day had arrived. It was a typical day for me, honestly, at least when I did readings. It was one scheduled after another.

It wasn't until the end of the day before I was able to call LaDonna back.

"Hey, Joanna."

"Hi, LaDonna. Sorry it's taken so long to get back to you. Busy day."

"No problem. It just means I have some more news for you. Three more offers came in."

"Wait. What? It hasn't even been for sale for a full day yet."

"I know, but when people found out it was your house, the offers have just been pouring in."

Of course, that's the reason.

She ran through the offers for me. "So what do you want to do?"

"Accept whoever wants to close the quickest so I can get out of there."

Money didn't matter as much as speed in this case. They were all solid, and they were all over the asking price, so that wasn't a concern. The one that could close the quickest would be the winner here.

"Great! I'll let you know."

Just like that, my house was sold, and I could finally move on to a new chapter in my life. Well, in a few weeks or so once we could set the closing dates and move.

Chapter Twenty-Five

~Joanna~

With this move, I decided to hire a professional moving company to come in and pack, load the truck, and move it across town for me. I wanted no repeat of my last moving day experience. Al was still recovering from the shooting and would likely have months still to go.

Not only that, but it was also my entire house, minus the office stuff, and it was a little too much to ask friends and family to help pack and move. Though I had plenty of help today.

Audrey and Stan were helping me coordinate the move. Someone had to be at each house to supervise and sign off on the movers. So they would be at the new home waiting while I ensured that the old place got packed up and loaded.

Tessa and Ruby were keeping both Oakley and Chewy for me. The twins had gone back to college.

Micah and Josh came to help as well. Even though I'd hired people, they said it was mainly moral support.

"And you can always use extra hands, boss."

As I watched the moving truck drive away, I felt a weird empty feeling. I turned to face my now empty house. The place I bought by myself after digging myself out of debt. It was a symbol of my freedom from the financial burden, from my lying late husband, and from a life I didn't want to go back to.

I looked to my friends standing nearby. "I brought my daughter to this home and have raised her here for the past eight months. She learned to crawl right there and pulled up for the first time over there."

I would miss it so much, but the memories of the break-ins, the threats, the kidnappings were too fresh and too scary to stay.

Micah put his arms around me as a few tears fell.

"It's okay," he said softly. "You'll make new memories in the new house."

"I know."

As we walked out of the front door for the last time, Marcy Dalton, my neighbor and one of my mom's friends, was coming up the walkway.

"I'm so glad I didn't miss you," she said. "Here. I made you these."

She handed me a container with cookies inside. No doubt her famous oatmeal raisin.

"Oh, Marcy, thank you."

"I'm so sorry that you have to move. It has been a joy to have you here."

It hadn't always been a joy for me to have my mom's friend spying on me and reporting back to my mother, but I simply smiled and gave her a hug.

With that, I took one final look at the house. Then, sighing, I slowly turned to face Micah and Josh. I nodded, and we headed over to my new life in my new home.

When we got over to the new house, I could see that the movers were working fast. The truck was nearly half empty. Micah and Josh jumped in to help the movers with unloading.

I headed inside to see how things were going. Audrey and Stan were directing workers to the various rooms. Before long, the house was a cardboard paradise.

"Want us to start unpacking?" Stan asked, pocketknife in hand, ready to start opening boxes.

I surveyed the messy living room. I couldn't bring Oakley home to this. She was just starting to pull up and would be pulling things over on herself.

"Yeah, if y'all have time to help, that would be great."

"Absolutely." Stan cut into the first box.

Micah and Josh went to my room to put my bed together.

Audrey and I went to Oakley's room.

Two hours later, both bedrooms were done, the living room and dining rooms were mostly put together, and the kitchen was about halfway. However, we all needed a break.

"I'll order some pizza," I said.

"Let's go sit outside," Josh suggested.

We all headed out to the front porch, where my patio furniture had been left. We pushed things around until we were all comfortably seated with a cold drink and waited for the pizza.

The guys started talking about the big game from yesterday. I wasn't even sure which teams were playing or what sport they were talking about.

"This is a cute neighborhood, Jo," Audrey said.

"Yeah, I love the charm of it," I said.

"I noticed it has a cute park."

"Yeah, it's not too far from here either. An easy walk over."

"I hope that you won't have as much trouble here as you did at the last place."

"Same. I'm hoping keeping the business and my home separate will help. I'll also be more careful when I come and go too."

"I have never, to my knowledge, been followed. I just can't imagine."

"It wasn't something I would have ever in a million years thought I'd have to worry about."

"You haven't told me anything new with Ted's murder. Any leads?"

"Well, all things seem to point to that group in Redlynne, but nobody knows who they are, which is weird, right?"

"I guess. Honestly, I didn't pay that much attention to that stuff until you got wrapped up in the Landon case and started working with Hank."

"I didn't either," I said. "I knew a little. Now I know way too much." I lowered my voice. "Did I tell you I broke into his file room a few weeks ago? Not long before I found this house."

"No, what the heck, Jo?"

"Okay, so maybe it wasn't exactly breaking in because Eddie just walked me in, but I wasn't supposed to be there. He said he would get in so much trouble for taking me there."

"Still, that's crazy. Did you find anything interesting?"

"A little, but nothing that pointed to anyone who could have murdered my husband. It's honestly a little frustrating, and I'm starting to think it wasn't murder."

"Yeah, it sounds frustrating," Audrey said, taking a sip of her water.

"But then I was going to go out to Redlynne, just to look around, and I stopped at the cemetery, just in case Ted was hanging around." I looked around, not sure of who might be listening outside of our little group. "Cecil was there."

"Oh, my..." Audrey moved to the edge of her seat.

"Yeah, and he told me he'd been trying to recruit Ted to work for him. That Ted had actually started to do some jobs for him."

"What?"

"Yes, so he said he wanted to set the record straight that it wasn't him. He hadn't remembered for sure the first time we met, but then later he had. He even had a picture of Ted from back then."

"Wow, Jo, just wow."

We didn't get to talk more as our pizza arrived. Instead, we ate it on the porch, enjoying the view of my front yard and new neighbors' houses.

It was quiet here, much like my other house. A few people walked by and waved, but this street didn't have much vehicle traffic, and there weren't a lot of children out, but I'd only been here for a few hours. So perhaps the kids were inside at the moment.

My hope was that Oakley would have neighborhood friends, and they would have playdates and sleepovers. I couldn't wait.

After pizza, Micah and Josh had to go. Audrey and Stan stayed another hour helping me, but they had to go get the boys from our parents.

Leaving me on my own for another hour before I gave up and went to get Oakley and Chewy. I couldn't wait to see them both settle in here.

Before I drove over, I did one lap around the inside of the house, checking that everything was, for the most part, baby-proofed. I was so proud of what we'd gotten done in one day. Of course, it wasn't perfect yet, but it was feeling a bit like home already.

I smiled and went to bring my little family home.

Chapter Twenty-Six

~Clint~

I finally got the call from my uncle, so I'd taken a rare day off to drive out to Redlynne. He was going to let me review his team's findings from the accident. He sounded strange, so I knew he must have found something.

My dad had been excited to hear that I'd been speaking to his youngest brother. He'd always hated that we didn't get along better.

I didn't tell anyone what exactly I was doing, except for Terry. He'd been the one to suggest talking to Doug, so here I was now, halfway between Creekview and Redlynne.

I was listening to my favorite history podcast. It distracted me from thinking about Joanna and her late husband and if old Uncle Doug was going to talk to me as an equal or a dumb kid.

An hour later, I was rolling into town. I hadn't been here in several years. However, it had changed quite a bit. The once small-town feeling was gone, replaced with modern and trendy. My single side immediately noticed the many gastropubs, clubs, and bars, perfect for taking a date or meeting a new lady.

While the thought of meeting new women, ones that my mother hadn't vetted for me, was appealing, it was a bit of a hike to come out here just for a date.

If I wanted to dip my toe in this dating pool, it would mean a move. Not something I was looking for or wanting at the moment.

I loved Creekview. I loved the department I worked for, and I wasn't in a place mentally that I wanted to make a move. Plus, moving over here would mean reporting to my uncle, which was not something I wanted to do.

Before I headed over to meet the chief of police, I made my way from the hip main drag over to the area where Ted had died. Not that I expected to see any clues, but getting a lay of the land and understanding the types of buildings around it might help when reading the reports.

I noted that the landscape changed. While the streets closer to the shopping and restaurants had heavy traffic, the roads here were nearly empty. I might have seen two other vehicles by the time I pulled up to the vacant printing company where the accident happened.

I parked near an empty parking lot across from the abandoned building. I stepped out of my truck and scanned the area. From the couple of images I'd seen online, this looked like the spot.

I couldn't see any security cameras, but as I've found in my line of work, sometimes they blend in. I walked to the end of this block and looked back toward my truck. It was a straight road with not many obstacles or things to hit. The buildings were set back far enough, and in this immediate area, there were no light poles or other structures.

From my limited knowledge about the accident, it happened right in the middle of the road.

That seemed strange. Not something I'd noticed in the few pictures I'd seen. In my experience, accidents didn't usually cause death under these conditions.

Of course, that doesn't mean it wasn't possible. It was. Anything was possible with one moment of inattention, a little bit of speed, or a few too many drinks, sure. Though this was enough that it should have been examined closely to rule out foul play. At least, that's what Walden and I would do if this happened in Creekview.

Perhaps Joanna was on to something with this. Damn, I didn't want to admit she really could speak to the dead.

I crossed the street to continue to look for any clue that could help me understand how this accident might have happened or if there were things I was missing. Looking at various angles, I saw nothing that stuck out.

From where I stood, I could hear voices inside the warehouse. I'd thought it was vacant, but I guess not.

I shrugged and continued my walk to the other end of the street, looked back up the road that I'd just surveyed, and then crossed back over to the side where my truck was parked.

Reaching my truck, I did another scan of the area, and this time I noticed a figure standing in an upper window. They seemed to watch me for a moment before appearing to back away slowly. Hard to tell what was really happening with just a silhouette.

"Strange," I thought.

I climbed back in my truck, taking one final look before driving to the police station.

Arriving, I parked in the visitor lot and headed in. The building was newer than our station, but stepping in, there was the same familiar vibe. Lots of people milling around the lobby area, likely waiting for someone to be released or to speak with an officer about a report.

I messaged my uncle that I was there as I waited my turn to speak to the officer behind the reception desk.

"Name?" he said when it was my turn.

"Detective Clint Hartley."

"Hartley? Are you related to the Chief?"

"He sure is. This little pipsqueak is my nephew." The booming voice of my uncle said from behind me.

I was mildly offended by the pipsqueak comment considering I was three inches taller, but he did have at least twenty pounds more on him.

"Well, I'll be, Chief. Police work run in the family?"

"Nah, just the two of us," Chief Hartley said. "You ready, kid?"

"Sure," I said.

I followed him back through the bullpen of officers. They all turned to watch us walk by. Some greeted him. Others whispered. This right here is one of the reasons why I'd hated to ask Doug for help.

We walked into his office. It looked a lot like the chief's office at my station, but less paperwork on the desk. They must do more electronic files than we do. I was ready for us to move in this direction. Unfortunately, paper got damaged and lost too easily.

"Alright, so you want to know what we found?"

"Yeah, that would be nice." I mean, that was the reason I drove two hours after all.

"It definitely looks like foul play. The side of the vehicle had damage consistent with another car bumping against it as if trying to push them off the road."

"Shit."

"Yeah."

"Any ideas?" I asked.

"My guess, and mind you, it's only a guess at this point, those witnesses had something to do with it. The problem, two are missing, and the third appears to be a fake name."

"I thought you said they were in jail."

"They were. At least the two that are missing now were. They were released recently and didn't report to their parole officer. Our searches for them have not turned up any results yet."

"Any ideas on where they are?"

"None. If they're alive, they're with their gang. If dead, well then they could be anywhere."

"I was going to ask about interviewing them, but clearly, that's not an option," I said. "You'd also mentioned a toxicology report had been done on the victims. What did that turn up?"

"The one that had been filed with the fake report showed alcohol and drugs in their systems, but we found the actual results after some digging. Nothing. Both clean."

I sat back in the chair, letting the full impact of his words hit me. Joanna had been right, or at least close. They had possibly been murdered.

"But why do the actual autopsy if they were just going to fake it?"

"Right. I thought of that, but honestly, I have no answer."

The only thing I could come up with is that someone not on the gang's payroll had done the real one, and then it was replaced with the fake when filed. I mean, the last part is obviously what happened.

"I drove over to the scene before coming here."

"Oh yeah, see anything interesting?" he asked.

"Well, I noticed the spot of the accident was in the middle of a straight road. No curves or turns, nothing that should have caused a crash that would kill them both. I mean, it could happen, but the odds are less in those conditions."

"Yeah, I'd thought the same."

"What do you know about the buildings around there? Who owns them?"

"Not much. As you noticed, most are long abandoned. I think they're owned by the same holding company."

"A holding company? Not a property management firm?"

"Yeah, I know. It looks a tad suspicious, but it looks like the holding company has several property management companies that it has a stake in, so I assume one of those actually owns the property. I'm still trying to unravel the structure of it."

"Any ties to this Redlynne gang I've heard so much about?"

"You heard about them, huh?" I nodded, so he continued. "Yeah, we think it might be, but they've mostly been quiet to date."

I thought about Hank. From what I was told, he'd started out quiet too, slowly building up his business. He owned Hammersley Holdings as well as multiple property management companies and helped several small businesses get off the ground by investing in their owners.

I didn't know much about Cecil Edwards. He was still fairly new like this group, only starting a few years before them. But from what I'd heard, he'd tried to model Hank's business. It was a successful business, so I could understand why others would want to copy it.

"Nothing else about it?"

"No, why?"

"It looks empty, but there were people in it today."

"Hmm." He rubbed at the stubble on his face. "Not really that unusual though, is it?"

I shrugged. Probably not, but I had a gut feeling something wasn't right about that place. The voices sounded normal, nothing suspicious in that. I was likely overly paranoid at this whole situation, mainly since Joanna was involved, and I knew she'd already had far too much attention in this.

"You'd mentioned I could review the reports. Is that still a possibility?"

"Sure. Let's go next door to the conference room, and I'll pull it up on the screen in there."

He grabbed a laptop as we stood to go to the other room. He hooked up his computer to the projector and was able to pull everything up digitally.

"How do you like this digital format?" I asked him.

"It was tough to get used to in the beginning. I'm an old-fashioned guy. I like paper, but for times like this, it is so much easier to share. No more photocopies or passing a single copy around for everyone to share."

I would have to talk to my chief and get some support around going digital. Most of the other officers would likely back me up on this. It was a hot button item for most of us.

Together we went through each report, both the false one and then new versions from his team.

"You can see the differences between the two."

"Yeah, it's obvious this one is faked, just by the little I know about the crash scene."

"That's why nearly the whole department was fired and replaced." He said. "So what're ya gonna do with this info?"

"I'm not sure. I assume you're not planning to reopen the case."

"Don't plan on it, but I could be talked into it."

"I haven't talked to Joanna about this yet, but I think she wants closure on it." I thought of Monica. At least I knew how she passed. Shot in the line of duty while on a domestic violence call that went sideways quickly.

"Alright then. Just let me know." He shut the laptop, and we said our goodbyes.

As I drove home, I thought of Monica again. I missed her, but if I were honest with myself, I'd already forgotten the sound of her voice. I couldn't remember what her perfume smelled like, and I couldn't hear her voice any longer in my dreams.

Why was I holding on so tightly to her when she'd already been gone so long?

On the flip side, I could hear Joanna's voice, could picture her clearly. She was real, and she was alive.

I sighed and turned the radio up to not think about either lady for the remainder of the long drive home.

Chapter Twenty-Seven

~Joanna~

I put out the spinach dip and spread the crusty slices of bread all around it on the plate.

"And done," I said to Oakley, who was watching me from her pack-n-play.

She giggled her reply.

"Thanks. I think it looks nice as well."

Tonight, we were hosting a housewarming party. Guests should be arriving any minute. I scanned the dining room area and the connecting kitchen. Everything did look good. I'd been preparing food most of the day.

Plus, I couldn't wait to show off my new house. I'd unpacked the last box three days ago, and I had it decorated mostly the way I wanted it. A few months ago, I couldn't have pictured anywhere feeling as much like home as my other house, but only two weeks here, and I couldn't even imagine living anywhere else.

I'd kept the guest list somewhat small. Micah and Josh, Tessa and Ms. Ruby, plus my entire family. I'd also invited Laney Landon, and despite how busy we'd both been lately, she was one of my best friends. Then last but not least, I'd invited Janie.

I'd decided not to invite any of Hank's men, like Al or Eddie. Even though I considered them both friends, I felt it was best to keep that part of my life away from my new home. I might have them over someday, but for now, I kept my guest list on the smaller side.

Chewy sprinted to the door and gave one bark just as there was a knock.

"Hey, guys, come on in." It was Audrey, Stan, and their two boys. I hugged my sister and welcomed them in.

"Looks great, Jo," Audrey said, stepping inside. "You've really gotten settled in since I was last here."

"Thanks. Yeah, it's been a lot of work, but it's feeling like home."

Next to arrive was Janie and then Tessa. Soon after, the rest of the guests arrived. I smiled, looking at the faces of my favorite people as they all visited and ate.

Laney had put Aspen in with Oakley, and the two half-sisters were chatting it up while also pulling at each other's clothes, hair, and ears.

"They sure have grown," she commented when she saw me watching them.

"They have."

"Have you talked to Jeremy lately?" A slight sadness in her tone. Jeremy was her late husband and both girls' father. He was dead and had been the first person I'd talked to in the afterlife since I was a child.

"Not recently. It's been a month or more."

She frowned and nodded. "I saw that Cate's trial will start soon."

"Yeah, I hope she ends up at Carter. It's the closest facility."

"That would be good," she said. "Have you seen her recently?"

Laney knew I visited her and that we'd kept in touch.

"I did visit her not that long ago. She looked good. Not like her former bubbly, shiny self, but still good, considering."

"That's good. I worry about her sometimes."

"I do too, but she seems to be doing okay."

My youngest nephew, Dylan, ran up and hugged me.

"I lovey your new house, Auntie Jo," he said.

"Thanks, I do too."

He then quickly ran off to his dad, who hoisted him up, giving him a little tickle as he did. Dylan giggled, then threw his arms around Stan's neck.

I smiled. This was perfect. I'd been so worried that this place wouldn't mean as much as my last, but I think this one would mean more in some ways. The image of my nephew enjoying himself was going to be one of my first memories of my new house.

I made the rounds, trying to mingle with everyone. I gave my mom the most attention as I knew it would mean a lot.

She'd gone and picked up Oakley and was talking to her.

"Do you like your new home, Oakey?" she asked.

Oakley babbled away, I assume telling her all about our day.

"Oh really? Well, your mom has tried to make it a nice place for you."

Did my mom just compliment me? I thought I might faint.

"Mom, that's so sweet. Thank you."

"Now, if you would stop putting yourself and my beautiful granddaughter in danger and get a real job, you wouldn't have to make so many unnecessary changes in your life."

There it is. That's the mom I knew.

"Yeah, well, you know me, Jo thrill-seeker." I rolled my eyes and looked for my sister. We locked eyes and had a private, secret sister conversation.

"Oh, Jo, don't be so dramatic. You know what I mean."

She always said this after she'd offended me. I almost never knew what she meant, but I let it go.

"Do you need anything? Another drink, perhaps?"

"No, I'm fine. I have my favorite girl right here, and that's all I need."

I moved on quickly, finding Micah looking sheepish in the kitchen.

"Hey, Mic, what's up? You okay?"

He blushed. "Yeah, I'm... I'm going to propose to Josh. I'm so nervous."

I squealed as quietly as possible. "Oh, that's so exciting! When?"

"Tonight. Here." He smiled. "If that's okay. I figure most of the important people are here, and he won't expect a thing."

"Wait, what about a ring? Do you... do that?" I felt a little silly asking him, but I didn't know how it worked.

"We actually talked about it in the past and decided when we were ready, we wouldn't use a ring, though I thought about it. We will actually pick out custom bands together later."

"Oh, I love that, but what about your parents or his?"

"It's okay. I actually talked to both his and mine. They know it's coming soon."

"Oh, good. I'm so happy that you picked to do it here."

"I'm glad you don't mind. I was worried the most about you thinking I was stealing your thunder." He squeezed my hand.

"Not at all! I love that you want to do it tonight." I looked across the room to where Josh was standing, completely unaware of his partner's plan. "It just adds another beautiful memory to my new home."

"Thanks, boss." He leaned over, giving me a hug and kissing the top of my head. "I think I'm ready."

He moved across the room, took Josh's hand, and then cleared his throat to get everyone's attention.

"Josh, darling, we have been friends for years, lovers for two, and in so many ways committed to each other for life." He smiled and moved to one knee. Josh gasped and started fanning himself a little. "But I'd like to ask if you would commit once more by becoming my husband?"

The crowd waited quietly to hear the answer, except for Harris and Dylan, who asked what was happening. Audrey had to shush them.

"Oh, babe, of course I will," Josh giggled.

The crowd cheered as the couple sealed the engagement with a sweet kiss. As the kiss ended, everyone took turns congratulating the couple.

"I'm so happy for you both," I said when it was my turn. "There's almost no better couple I know."

"Thank you, boss," Micah said.

"I'm just still so shocked. I knew we would someday, but I was so surprised." We hugged.

Soon after this, the party started to break up. Tessa and Ms. Ruby stayed to help me clean up after the rest of the guests had left.

"I'm so happy for Micah and sweet Josh," Ms. Ruby commented as she rinsed dishes.

"Me too. They're perfect together," I said.

"Now, if we could find you two ladies someone," Ms. Ruby said with a chuckle.

"Oh, you're one to talk, Mom," Tessa teased. "You haven't been on a date since Dad died three years ago."

"That's what you think."

"What?" Tessa and I said in unison.

She just grinned, giving us a wink as she finished the dishes.

"Mom, no, you can't just say that and then smirk at us."

"Yeah, Ms. Ruby, spill it," I said.

"It's really nothing. I recently met someone, and it's been going... nice."

"Who? When? I see you all the time."

"We've had a couple of lunch dates. Nothing serious."

"But you want it to be," I said. It was written all over her face.

"Oh, yeah, I wouldn't mind. He's a sweet man. A little older, but heck, I'm old now. All I'm going to meet is old men." She laughed. "He is a widower too."

"Oh, Mom, that's nice. I'm glad you found someone." Tessa hugged her mother.

"See? Now we have to get you ladies men."

"I'm happy being single," Tessa said quickly.

I stayed quiet, unsure if I was happy single or not. There were definitely times I missed having someone special.

I watched the mother and daughter share the sweet moment. I'd always been jealous of their connection. It was what I wanted with my mother but never had. I hoped to create this with Oakley so at least she might know this type of relationship.

Once the house was back to normal, or at least close enough, they said their goodbyes, and then it was just me.

I did hope I found someone again. I missed having that person to share my life with, plus I wanted to have more children. I'd even adopt again as it had been a wonderful experience.

My cell phone rang. The display read an unknown caller. I hesitated to answer it, but in the end, I did.

"Hello?"

"Don't think just because you moved, we can't find you," the deep voice threatened. The same voice that had called with the other threats. "We have our ways."

From outside and through the phone, I heard a car engine roar loudly and tires squeal. This caused Chewy to startle awake and run to the front door barking wildly. Thankfully, the car sound moved down the street and away from my house.

I quickly hung up, throwing my phone onto the couch. I ran to Oakley's room. Chewy stopped barking and followed me closely. Watching my daughter sleep peacefully in what I thought would be a safe home, away from the dangers of the outside world, I cried softly.

Oh, I'd been naïve to think whoever was after me wouldn't find me.

I'd have to ask Stan to finish the security system on my house tomorrow. It needed to be in place before I slept another night here.

I looked at my daughter once more before going to ensure all the windows and doors were locked. Then, retrieving my cell phone, I went to bed for what I assumed would be a long, sleepless night.

Chapter Twenty-Eight

~Joanna~

I was feeding Oakley her breakfast of yummy baby cereal with pureed pears. We were having a rousing conversation all about dogs, which happened to be her favorite thing in the world. She'd started pointing to them on our walks, and of course, our good boy, Chewy.

"What do you want to do after breakfast?" I asked her.

"Dawg."

"You want to play with Chewy?" He raised his head, giving his tail a wag in reply.

"Dawg!" She clapped and looked at him.

"Okay, we'll play with the dog."

I wiped the spoon over her chin to grab a bit of mush that had spilled out of her open mouth and then wiped the spoon on a paper towel. Then, grabbing a fresh spoonful, I offered it. She grinned and then opened her mouth.

"Good girl."

She clapped.

I loved moments like this. A quiet Sunday morning, just my girl and my dog. Though I hated that last night, my peace of mind had been ruined by one phone call and an unknown car.

The housewarming party had been perfect, including Micah and Josh's engagement. Family and friends together, laughing and making memories.

Then in one moment, it was shattered. After that, it had been a long night of me pacing and checking that the doors were still locked. I'd dozed a bit, but any noise woke me up.

The only reason I got any sleep was having Chewy near me. When I'd look over at him, his body was relaxed, and he'd be snoring away, which meant the coast was clear.

I'd already messaged Audrey this morning with a request for Stan's time today. She replied with sure and an offer to bring lunch and my nephews. I agreed. They'd be over in a few hours.

Oakley finished her breakfast, so I put her on the floor while I cleaned up her chair and bowl. Then I joined her for some playtime.

While we were playing, we had an unexpected visitor.

"Ted, hey, what're you doing here?" I asked with surprise as he materialized in the room.

"I'd heard through the grapevine that you'd moved. So I had to ask a lot of others how to find you. Finally got here." He looked around. "This is nice, but what happened with the other place?"

"Too many threats and bad memories."

"Threats?"

"Um, yeah, because I've been asking around about you, I guess."

"Wow, I thought that might happen, but given the amount of time since... I just thought it would give us both peace of mind knowing who did it and so you'd know the truth about how I died."

"Speaking of truth, you lied to me."

"I did a little, but I already came clean about working for Hank and why I was out of town."

"That's not what I'm talking about. Cecil told me he was trying to recruit you and that you were doing a job for him, not Hank, that night."

"No, I wasn't. He thought I was, but that was a job for Hank. Cecil had wanted me, that part's true."

"If that's true, then one, why did you not tell me that? And two, why would he lie to me?"

"Because that's what he does, and why would I tell you about Cecil wanting me to work for him? It wasn't like I was or even planned to."

"Well, you told me he was the one that murdered you or ordered the hit or whatever."

"Yes, because he was mad that I wouldn't work for him. Maybe he wanted to take out the competition."

"He also said that you were really good at making money. If that was the case, why were we in so much debt? Couldn't you have done whatever it was to make more?"

"Because it's illegal. I'm good at finding the loopholes and cleaning money."

I stared at him. He was laundering money. I'd already known that from Cecil and Eddie, but hearing him say it, I lost so much respect for him. He'd gone to college for finance and accounting. Was that what he took away from it?

"Look, Jo, for what it's worth, I'm sorry. All of that was dumb, stupid, and if I had it to do over, I wouldn't. Instead, I'd take a corporate job and wear the suit and tie, commute, the whole thing."

That didn't make me feel any better about what I'd learned, but I decided to just let it go. There was no point in continuing to rehash the same things over and over. It didn't matter in the grand scheme of things. He was dead. We weren't married any longer, and except for this potential murder, I didn't care about the rest of his lies. It really didn't matter at all.

"Thanks," I mumbled.

We were silent for several minutes. Oakley was playing, crawling, and pulling up on everything around me. She was used to me randomly talking. She, of course, didn't understand or know that I saw ghosts, and that's who I was almost always talking to, but she was used to it.

"Wow, your daughter is getting big."

"Thanks, she is. She'll be a year old in a few months."

More silence as the baby played all around us.

"Well, I'm sorry for all the trouble I've caused for you." He flashed a sheepish smile. "Don't worry about this anymore. I'm happy that I've gotten to tell my side of the story, whether you believe it or not."

"I believe you." Maybe if I said it out loud, I'd actually believe it too. Telling a small lie to a ghost didn't seem like a big deal, especially after all the whoppers he'd told me.

"Good." He paused. "I should go. Not sure when or if I'll see you again, but thanks."

That was it. He left. I suddenly felt empty and alone. A feeling you would think I'd be used to, but he had been someone that I had a history with, shared so many laughs and love with. Now I knew it was final.

Closure should have brought relief, but this didn't feel complete. Instead, it felt hollow and lonely. This wasn't what I'd wanted to give others.

That's why my tagline was a Medium with a Heart. I tried to give people love, hope, and peace. I put my heart into each reading and hoped they took away a positive, cheerful vibe.

So many had said they had. I'd only had a few unhappy folks over the years. One lady had hoped her husband would reveal some hidden riches, but as it was back in my faking it days, there was no way I could make that up. So I told her that he'd said there weren't any accounts. Honestly, I had no idea. For all I knew, there was unclaimed money for him out in the world.

I sighed heavily, looking at the spot where Ted had exited. Would I ever have peace in this? Would I ever know the truth about his life and his death? I highly doubted it.

I shook off thoughts of him and turned all my attention to the baby. She was cruising around the couch and looking at me for approval.

"Good girl! You are getting so big."

She clapped, which meant letting go of the couch. She stood there for a few seconds. That could only mean walking wasn't too far in our future.

"Oh, Oakley, you are standing!" I clapped.

She grinned and then went back to holding the furniture and walking around.

Later, Audrey and her family arrived. The boys came bursting in, yelling for Oakley. She squealed and crawled toward them. Harris dropped in front of her and immediately started a one-sided conversation with her. Though she did try to reply, it was mostly chatter at this point, with an almost word mixed in.

"Aw, that is so sweet," Audrey said. "It's what I'd imagined when I thought of cousins for the boys."

"They are so good with her," I said, watching as Harris held a toy for her.

Not being much older than Oakley, Dylan wasn't quite as gentle or sure of his role. Instead, he just tried to mimic his older brother.

Stan followed them in, loaded down with his toolbox and the new security system. He dropped a kiss on my cheek and then set his things down in the living room.

Audrey had stopped at our favorite deli for some sandwiches and pasta salad. I had chips and cold drinks to go with it. We got everything unpacked. She fixed a plate for each of her boys and then called them to the table.

The boys chatted happily while we all ate. Stan cracked jokes, which caused the boys to laugh. Oakley watched and giggled along with them.

After lunch, Stan went right to work on my security cameras. Then I fixed Audrey and me a cup of hot tea and brought it into the living room so we could watch the kids and visit.

It was on the tip of my tongue to talk to her about Ted, but with the boys here, I didn't want them to overhear and repeat anything. So instead, we just talked about the kids, our parents, my new house.

"Your housewarming last night was nice," she commented.

"Yes, and I'm so happy for Micah and Josh."

"Me too! Did you know he was going to do that?"

"Yeah, he'd talked to me about it just before he did it. I was thrilled to hear."

"Any hints at when they'll set the date?"

"I haven't talked to him about plans yet. But I'm sure they'll announce it soon."

She lowered her voice and moved a little closer to me. "Any ideas about the call last night?"

I watched the children for a moment as I thought about who I thought it could be. Cecil had talked to me recently, so unless one of his men went rogue, I don't think it was him.

"I'm not sure, but I think it's related to Ted's death."

"Really? How or maybe why do you think that?"

"Well, you know I told you he thought he was murdered." I mouthed the last word so the boys wouldn't hear. "I have been doing some asking around about it."

"So you think it could be his murderer?"

"I think it is at least related somehow."

I'd already told her most everything, so I filled her in on Ted stopping by this morning.

"I can't believe how he tries to spin everything, and honestly, I have no idea who to believe. I just know that I didn't know Ted at all."

"Wow, Jo, wow." She sat back. "I honestly don't know what to say."

We moved on to other topics. I really didn't want to think about Ted anymore.

In the middle of the visit, I put Oakley down for a nap, and Dylan fell asleep on the extra bed in her room. Harris played a game on Audrey's phone.

Stan stuck his head inside. "Okay, think I'm done. Wanna come see?"

I followed him around the house as he explained to me what he'd done and where each camera was located.

"I put some in plain sight to hopefully deter some bad guys. Then others I hid a bit more to keep them from being tampered with, or as much as possible."

"Thanks. This looks good."

"Glad I could help," he said with a smile. "I was going to ask, would you mind watching the boys tonight? I'd love to take your sister out for dinner."

I hadn't watched them in a while, so it was about time I paid my sister and brother-in-law back for all their help.

"Of course! I would love to."

"Thank you!" He kissed the top of my head and then sprinted into the house. "Babe, we're having date night."

After they got things settled and all of Stan's tools loaded, they were off.

"Alright, Harris, it's just you, me, and the two little ones." They were both still asleep, though. "Got any ideas?"

"Can we watch a movie?"

"Sure. Sounds good."

We selected a movie, and soon Dylan joined us, still sleepy from napping. He climbed into my lap and giggled at the show.

Once Oakley was awake, I had started to regret my decision to watch them. I wasn't the mother that Audrey was. She had boys and nearly six years of experience. I had one tiny girl who was only nine months old.

The boys wrestled and ran and jumped all over. Chewy thought it was great fun, chasing them all over the house barking. This scared Oakley, but she soon caught on that it was just fun and games. Soon she was crawling behind them all, yelling and giggling.

Thankfully, though, that was as eventful as the night was, and by the time Stan and Audrey came back to get them, I felt like a pro and that I'd have no trouble sleeping that night.

Chapter Twenty-Nine

~Clint~

I was heading back into Redlynne to check on this property management company, the one that owned the printing company building. My gut said something wasn't right there.

I'd made an appointment with them to show me one of the properties nearby under the guise of a new tech company looking to expand from my house to an actual building.

Now to hope Uncle Doug didn't catch me snooping around his town. No telling what he'd say or do if he did.

I pulled into a visitor spot in front of the main office of Janssen Property Services. It was located a few blocks from downtown in the newly revitalized area of town that was full of fancy boutiques and gastropubs.

As I entered, I was greeted by a chipper receptionist. She looked to be my mom's age and had a bright smile and purple hair. My mom had not yet tried the colored hair thing, though I knew a few ladies who had.

"Hi, welcome. How can I help you?" The nameplate read Diane.

"Hi, Diane. I have an appointment."

"Your name?" She smiled at me.

"Seth. Seth Johnson." I lied. I hated lying, but I tried to remind myself of the goal here.

She typed into the computer. "Ah, yes, I see you here. Please have a seat, and I'll let Martin know you're here."

"Thanks."

I took a seat across from Diane's desk so I could see both the front door and the door leading to the offices. Nothing suspicious looking here. It looked like a typical waiting room with the standard lobby chairs, generic artwork, and fake plants.

I scrolled through my phone to entertain myself while I waited, which thankfully was only a few minutes before Martin, the leasing agent, came to get me.

"Seth?" he said, stepping into the lobby. I nodded. "Great. Follow me on back."

I followed him down the hall to a simple office. It had a view of the parking lot and not much else.

"So, you're interested in the old fabric building."

"Fabric?"

"Yeah, they used to produce fabrics. Mostly for furniture, I believe."

"Ah, okay. Interesting history, I'm sure."

"Yeah, it was owned by an Italian immigrant who came over in the 1920s. His family owned it until about five or six years ago. Then we bought it. We haven't leased it out yet. Just haven't found the right business."

"And you think my tech company could be it?"

"Maybe. That all depends on you."

Was that a threat, or was I just on edge from my lies? Of course, I'd practiced this and did a lot of homework on the subject, so I'm sure I could fake my way through it, but still, it wasn't what I usually did.

"Well, I brought my business model, as requested." I handed him the fake documents. "I have only five employees now, but looking to expand as we're growing the business and getting more clients."

"You said it's a technology company?" he asked, flipping through the folder I gave him.

I still didn't understand why they'd need to see that, but I guess to ensure it wasn't a fly-by-night type of operation. It took me a lot of research and hours to put those fake documents together.

"That's right. We're kind of like a think tank. People bring us their ideas for apps, and we turn it into reality."

"Uh, interesting." He looked back down at the paperwork. Then, when he got to the end, he looked up at me with a smile. "Ready to go see it?"

"Sounds good."

We walked out to the parking lot.

"Want me to drive?" he offered.

"Sure, then I won't get lost." Of course, I wasn't supposed to know my way around, so this went along with the lie. The truth was I'd already driven past the building before my appointment.

I followed him to a dark sedan with dark tinted windows.

"Nice car," I commented as I climbed in.

"Business has been good." He smirked.

He gave me a tour of the town as we drove over, pointing out new restaurants or businesses and other properties that the company managed.

As we passed the printing company, he was silent. It was the only place he didn't point out to me, so I decided to probe.

"That almost looks like an old printing company. The exterior looks intriguing. I bet it has a great story."

"Oh, yeah, it is. Used to print the newspaper for Redlynne. Now it's empty, but it's still got some of the equipment inside."

"Oh yeah, I'd love to see that," I commented. "Do you know who owns it?"

He cleared his throat and looked around. "Um, we do."

"Is something wrong with it?"

"No, it's just not for lease at the moment."

"Why not? It looks like it could be a great space."

"Upper management has other plans for it." He'd broken out into a sweat and was darting his eyes around. What was he so nervous about? Clearly, my hunch was correct. Something was going on in that building.

We finally arrived at the fabric building. It was only two blocks from the printing company. Nothing special about it. The entire building had been cleaned out with no remaining hint of its former life.

"I do like the exposed bricks," I commented.

"Yeah, that's a favorite of most people."

I faked my way through some questions, answered his, and then thanked him for his time. Then we drove back to his office and parted ways with me saying I'd let him know what I decided. My plan was to say that we'd found another space.

I climbed into my truck but noticed that Martin didn't get out of his car. Instead, he drove out of the parking lot and took a right, so I decided to follow him.

I trailed him for several blocks, trying to keep my distance so he didn't notice me. Then finally, we made our way back to the block with the printing company on it. Since this area didn't have much traffic, I had to hang back quite far and then stopped short of following him down the road, but I knew right where he was going.

I circled back, trying to give him time to get out of his car and go inside. Sure enough, as I drove past, I saw his car in the parking lot along with two others.

I knew something was going on here. Was he going to tattle that I'd asked questions, or was he meeting for other reasons?

Either way, my suspicion of Janssen Property Services was right. They were a front for something, and if my hunch was correct, they were behind Ted's murder as well. At this point, though, it was just a gut feeling from my discussions with Uncle Doug and my limited investigation.

Satisfied with my findings, I pointed my car toward home. I'd have a couple of hours to think about my next move. Did I let Doug know or let Joanna in on the fact I was following leads?

As long as Joanna wasn't in danger, I'd have time to look into it. Nobody else was being threatened, and since I hadn't heard from her again, I assumed she was doing okay.

Though I did hear she sold her house and moved across town. I hadn't reached out yet. My feelings for her were still fresh, and the empty pit in my stomach at the mere thought of her reminded me why I tried to keep my dating casual.

I shook the memories of her and cranked up the radio to drown out any more thoughts of her for the rest of the drive back to Creekview.

Chapter Thirty

"He says that he's sorry for your last conversation and that the fight was irrelevant in the grander scheme of things." I looked over at Mr. Moore, and he nodded. Then I smiled at his widow.

I really enjoyed my new office space. It had been a few weeks now, and I'd gotten good feedback from all the families and readings so far. The Moores were my third appointment for today. I'd have one more after this, and then it was the end of the day, and I could get home to Oakley.

"It really was a silly fight, but who knew you'd have a heart attack just hours later." She dabbed a tissue to her eyes. "You have missed so much."

"I haven't missed anything. I've been right there by your side, just as I promised I'd be." I spoke for him as I typically did, often switching back and forth between speaking in the first and third person. I judged the situation on what I should do. "I saw when Jemma and Bob's baby was born. I was right there holding your hand."

Mrs. Moore smiled as a few fresh tears fell. She quickly dried them.

"I'm so glad you were there. Our first grandchild."

"And Benjamin is getting married soon. I'm so thrilled for him and Addy. They make a beautiful couple."

"He'll be so happy to hear that. He wanted your guidance when he was thinking about asking her. So I did the best I could to advise him."

"I was there and heard every word. You did wonderfully."

She choked on a laugh. "I'm so glad. I didn't know if I said everything quite like you would have."

"Well, we're almost out of time," I said, checking the time. "Any final words or questions?"

He looked at his wife. "Please tell her I will be by her side for every moment and for as long as I can."

I passed on the message to her, and then they both said goodbyes.

As I walked Mrs. Moore out to reception, I noticed Al was visiting with Tessa. He smiled at me.

"Well, thank you, Mrs. Moore. I hope you enjoyed your reading."

"Oh, I did. Thank you. I will definitely make another appointment in the future."

Mrs. Moore then selected my book and a coffee mug with our newest logo on it. She smiled at me as she handed them to Tessa.

I motioned for Al to follow me. Once we were away from the front office, I hugged him gently, as his arm was still in a sling from his gunshot.

"What're you doing here?" I asked.

"Checking on you."

"I'm fine." I laughed. "How are you feeling?"

"I'm healing."

Back in my office, I sat in one of the armchairs while he took the seat across from me.

"You've made this space very nice," he said, looking around. "But I knew you would."

"Thanks. I think it's a great move for us."

"How's the new house?"

"Oh, it's wonderful. I miss my old house at times, but this one is quickly becoming home."

"I need to get by to see it."

"Yes, you should." I smiled. "But that's not why you're here, is it?"

"No." He paused, adjusting his sling. "I've heard rumors that you've been snooping around our office."

"Shit." I didn't curse often, but when it was necessary, well, it spilled out. "Does Hank know?"

"I don't think so. You need to be more careful."

"I know. I know, but I needed to find out something, anything. He was my husband."

"I understand that, but I've already plucked you out of danger once, and while I would try my damnedest to make sure that you aren't in danger again, you have to help me out here."

"I know."

"Hank has warned the guys to stay out of this, and you could get Eddie in trouble for that stunt."

"How did you find out?"

"I was helping Hacker that night, and I noticed the fake loop footage. I stopped it to see what was going on. I'm also the one who tipped off Hacker about Hank being on his way there. He had no idea."

My mouth fell open. It had been weeks since that evening. I'd already house hunted and moved in, and now he came to tell me this.

"Why are you only telling me now? That was weeks ago."

"I've been a little busy myself." He motioned to his arm. "Plus, my mom and sisters take up a lot of my time when I'm not working. Besides..." He reached into his jacket, behind his sling, revealing a file folder. "I brought you this."

He handed me the folder. "It took me a while to put this together, but I think it's what you might be looking for."

My body started to hum with anticipation of what was in the file. Could it be answers? I took a deep breath and then looked at Al.

"Before I look, I have one question."

"What's that?"

"Cecil talked to me recently. He told me he was trying to recruit Ted to work for him."

"Not exactly a question, but I believe it, though I don't know for sure. Ted was great at what he did. Everyone wanted him." He nodded toward the file.

"I will, just one more question, maybe rhetorical, but if he was so good at his job, from what Cecil said, making money, then why did he leave me with such debt?"

"Because he was also horrible at gambling but thought he was better than he was. Plus, his ways of making money weren't legal, so it could have put you at even more risk had he done that for his household."

I sighed and opened the file folder. Inside were photocopies of ledgers, bank statements, and more of the receipt-like things that showed a job had been completed. I saw some of these when I was in Hank's file room.

I studied them a little closer because there was something here that Al wanted me to see. That's when I noticed the name. It wasn't Ted's name or even Hank's on these.

"Wait. Where did you get these?"

"I called in a few favors."

"Holy crap, Al." I flipped through a little more slowly now that I knew what I was looking at. "Wow, you must have been owed one big favor."

"You could say that." He reached into his jacket again. "Now before I give you this one, I must warn you, it's a little graphic."

I braced myself for what I might see in this next file. When I opened it, I noticed grainy screenshots.

"Are these from a security camera?"

"Yes."

I flipped through as the whole story played out in front of me. Images of Ted and Nicki's car coming down the street with another next to it, appearing to push it. The vehicle crashed into a pole. The next showed Ted being dragged from the car.

I fought back the tears as I kept flipping until the final few pictures, a familiar car pulling up at the scene. A man and woman appeared to run toward the car. She dropped beside it, hands to her face. The man looked to be yelling at the other men.

"Wait... wait. Is this?" I stared at Al.

"Yep, the Redlynne gang. These two are the heads, and those were their guys."

"Nooo..." The world around me went black.

Chapter Thirty-One

Yesterday had been a shocker. Finding out exactly who had killed my husband caused me to faint. Al had been a dear and ensured I was okay. Tessa brought me hot tea, and Micah hovered over me the rest of the day.

I would have canceled and gone home, but my next appointment had already arrived, so I did the reading and then went home. The whole night, I paced and muttered, trying to decide what to do with the information.

Today I was no closer to a decision on what to do. Should I tell Clint? Try to find Ted? Go to Hank?

No, not Hank. That might just get Al in trouble. I'd already caused enough for him by getting him shot. I also wanted to keep Eddie out of trouble. I'd already asked too much of him.

Since I now knew it wasn't Cecil, should I go to him? But that thought was short-lived as I knew he couldn't or wouldn't do anything. He only seemed to do something if it benefited him. There was nothing in this for him.

I didn't make a decision, deciding to table it for now. Simply knowing who it was should be enough, but also knowing who it was made it worse.

There was a knock at the door, and then Janie let herself in.

"Morning, Jo," she said.

"Hey, good morning."

Oakley made a beeline for her nanny, pulling up on her leg. Janie scooped her up.

"She ate cereal and apples about thirty minutes ago. Has a fresh diaper, and she slept well last night. Chewy has also eaten and been outside."

"Great."

I kissed Oakley and told her goodbye, then did my new commute to my office. I hated driving in traffic, but I loved having the time in the car to listen to a new podcast I'd recently found. It was paranormal stories. The narrators were excellent, really bringing the stories to life. It distracted me from the real-life decision I had to make or the genuine fear I had at knowing who the killers were.

I arrived at work in the middle of a good story, so I sat waiting for it to end. I probably looked crazy sitting in my car, leaning into the dash, and talking to myself as the story ended with a surprise ending.

"I did not see that coming," I said, turning off the car and getting out of the vehicle.

I'd been so focused on what I was doing, I hadn't noticed the strange car pull in behind me. I noticed it now as the two occupants stepped out, both with guns drawn.

"What the hell?"

It was Lydia and Calvin Murphy, of course, my ex-in-laws. How did they know how to find me? And did they know that I'd learned what they had done?

"You're coming with us," Lydia growled as she moved closer to me. She pointed the gun at me.

"Why?"

"Because it's time you pay."

"Pay? For what?"

"Ted's death." She snapped.

"That wasn't me. I was here in Creekview, a hundred miles away."

"It doesn't matter. It's still all your fault." Lydia said. "Now get in."

"No." I tried to run for the building. I'd reached the doors and saw Micah inside. "Get help!"

"But..."

"No, go. Get help."

At that moment, Calvin grabbed me from behind while Lydia shot at Micah. He ran through the building, and I could only hope out the back.

I fought, kicking and screaming all the way to the car, but Calvin was bigger and stronger, and soon he had me in the back seat. I tried to get out the other door, but it seemed to be child-locked.

Where was our security guard? I also didn't see Tessa's car yet.

He then reached in, trying to put handcuffs on me. Again, I fought as hard as I could to keep him from putting them on me, but again he won.

"I'm sorry, Jo. I'm really sorry." He whispered. His eyes were wide and watery. I knew he was scared of her and wouldn't help me no matter what.

Once he had the handcuffs on, he put a pillowcase over my head and pushed me down onto the seat.

"He got away," came Lydia's voice from next to the open door. "We need to get out of here before he reports us. I'll have Barney and Sam come to look for him."

They both jumped in, the doors slammed, and I could feel the car speed off. Lydia called her goons to come track down Micah.

"You close?" I heard her ask. "Yeah, good. He should still be close by."

I let the tears fall, but I tried to keep quiet. I didn't need to fuel Lydia's hate fire or give her any satisfaction that she was winning. Obviously, at this moment, she was winning whatever sick game this was.

I'd been kidnapped at gunpoint once before and by pure brute strength the second time, and while I'd been scared when Donovan had kidnapped me, it was in a hugely different way. Plus, he'd killed so many women before kidnapping me.

I don't remember being exactly scared when Cate had done it. She seemed frightened and confused herself, so I'd remained calm and talked to her normally.

This felt vastly different. Lydia had killed her favorite son, whether on purpose or accidentally. It didn't matter. To make things worse, she'd known about it when we planned his funeral, and still, she blamed me for whatever reason. That caused more tears to fall.

I could hear them talking in the front seat, but I couldn't quite make out their words. It sounded like they might be arguing, and Cal was on my side.

"You can't... this is wrong."

"... she knows... No turning back."

"We are going to get caught," Cal said. "... Not going down for..."

My mind was racing. What was I going to do? How could I get out of this one? I tried to calm my mind. No reason to panic. That wasn't going to do me any good. I needed to stay as levelheaded as possible if I was going to make it home.

I thought about Micah. I really hoped he'd been able to get somewhere safe and call for help. That was the only hope I had of being saved right now. I'm sure we were heading to Redlynne.

It was starting to get difficult to breathe inside the pillowcase, and I had no sense of time or direction. I may have even passed out for a while, but soon the car slowed, and by the crunching and pings on the underside of the vehicle, it sounded like we were on a gravel road.

I was trying to come up with a plan of what to do or what to say. Could I talk my way out of this? I knew the answer was no. This was Lydia

Murphy, after all. I'm not sure where all the hate toward me came from, but she'd always talked to me with disrespect and a nasty tone. Nothing I could say or do would change that.

After several minutes on this road, the car stopped, and there was some mumbling from the front before I heard car doors open, close, and one near me open. I was dragged roughly from the back and pushed forward.

We walked for several yards, or maybe it was miles. I had no sense of distance with the bag over my head, but it was finally ripped off. I blinked as the sunlight blinded me, following the near darkness of the car and pillowcase.

After my eyes adjusted, I realized we were in the middle of a field, nothing around us. However, I could see the car in the distance where the road had stopped.

I was pushed to my knees, Lydia standing over me. Calvin was back several paces, wringing his hands together and looking unsure of what to do.

"You. You are the reason my baby is gone," she said. "My baby boy."

"No, it wasn't me. I saw the footage, the pictures. It was you."

With animal-like reflexes, she lunged, backhanding me, which knocked me to the ground. I saw Cal take a step forward and then back.

I tried to sit up at least, but with my hands still cuffed, I couldn't quite.

"Stay down." She said, kicking me. "You know I told Ted to end things with you. He should have been with Paige, not you. He just wouldn't listen. I knew you were trouble the first time he brought you home."

She paced away from me, so I looked at Calvin. I mouthed help. He looked away and shifted his weight from one foot to the other and back.

"You weren't good enough for my Teddy. He was going to take over the family business, but you wanted a new house, a new car, new clothes. So he had to keep working for Hank."

"So you knew he worked for Hank? You knew what he did?"

"Who do you think taught him everything he knew?" She cackled. "He didn't learn that in school. Sure, he had to get that degree to make it look like he had a legit job, but no, he was educated in the family business."

"But why Hank?"

"So we could learn all his secrets and better understand how he ran things. We were still new back then, and we picked up a lot of great tips from old Hank the Hammer."

"Then why did you have him killed?"

"He wasn't supposed to be the target. That was a mistake," Lydia said. "We thought one of the other guys was going to be on that job. They had no business coming to Redlynne. That is our town."

"But you lived in Buckston, not Redlynne, at least back then."

"A cover. We're good at staying off the radar."

"Okay, but even if it was supposed to be someone else, wouldn't your guys know who he was, that he was your son?"

"Our guys didn't realize it was him at first, not until it was too late."

I saw some movement behind Cal and then motion to his other side. It was then that realization hit me. I was going to be rescued. The team was getting into position around us. I had to keep Lydia and Cal both focused on me.

"But why do you think it was my fault?"

"Because he had to keep you happy with all your fancy wants and needs."

"A house? Kids? Those are things people work toward when they're married. We didn't need top of the line, and he agreed to those things. Not a reason to be so angry. You have to have a better reason than that."

She let out the evilest laugh. "That was enough of a reason for me. Besides, it doesn't matter now. He is gone, and it's all your fault." She raised the gun, aiming it right at me. "Now something I've wanted to do for a very long time."

I squeezed my eyes shut just as Cal dove forward. That's when the bullets came from all around us. I laid as flat as I could on the ground. I could hear them hitting near me but kept my eyes shut tight. I didn't want to see what was happening. Hearing the screams and yelling was enough.

As quickly as it started, it was over. I slowly opened my eyes. The first thing I saw was Lydia's body lying in a pool of blood, Calvin next to her. They weren't moving. I choked out a sob.

Even though I hated them both, Lydia more than Cal, I didn't want that for their family, for them, or even for Ted. Did he know it had been his parents who had ordered the hit? He obviously knew they were the Redlynne gang, but why hadn't he told me? Yet another lie in a long line of them.

Al stepped forward along with Cecil. Eddie was digging in Calvin's pants, coming up a moment later with the key to the cuffs.

"Are you okay?" Al asked.

"I think so." But as they moved me to a sitting position, I noticed that my leg hurt. I looked down to see blood.

"You've been shot," Cecil said. He motioned to one of his guys, who ran over.

"It's not too bad. Looks like it just nicked you. A few stitches, and you should be good," the man said after he examined it.

"Thanks, umm?"

"Doc. I'm Doc."

"Thanks, Doc," I said.

They got the cuffs off of me and got me upright. I finally took in just who all was involved in my rescue. There was Al, Cecil, Doc, and Eddie, of course, but then I noticed Trent, Boomer, and Clint. He was standing talking to a guy I didn't recognize but who looked like he could be a brother or maybe a cousin.

Then rushing toward me now was Micah. He wrapped his arms around me, tears streaming down his face.

"I was so scared. I didn't even know who to call, so I called them all."

"Thank you," I choked out.

It had been a group effort and a coming together of sorts. I looked over at Clint. He smiled as a tear rolled down his face.

He came toward me as Micah let me go. When he reached me, he pulled me to him.

"I can't do this. I'm not strong enough, but I can't help it." He leaned forward, kissing me, a long passionate kiss that curled my toes. "I love you. I am so in love with you, Joanna."

"Oh, Clint... I love you too."

Chapter Thirty-Two

~Joanna~

It had been a week since my third kidnapping and rescue. My leg was healing from the gunshot wound. It needed more than stitches, and I'd be on crutches for a few more weeks, but I was safe, healing, and loved.

After his declaration, Clint and I had been nearly inseparable except for work. He said it was to help me with the baby while I was healing and on crutches. I definitely needed it since I couldn't carry Oakley well, but I could manage if I had to.

Though I suspected he wanted to keep an eye on me and possibly reconnect more intimately. You wouldn't hear me complain. I loved the help, and having him close by made me feel safe. Of course, with the Murphys' deaths, I felt safer anyway.

"I'm sorry we ended things after Donovan." He handed me a coffee cup.

"Me too. But good thing I got kidnapped again, so we got a second chance." I laughed.

"Not funny." He grinned and kissed me softly.

Oakley pulled herself up against the couch next to where he was sitting.

"Upp," she demanded.

He lifted her up and tickled her foot. "Better?"

She giggled and squirmed before settling into his lap. He'd quickly become one of her favorite people over the week. He was a fast learner when it came to baby care too. Of course, it helped that she wasn't a newborn anymore and had always been an easy baby.

Today neither of us had to work, and we were planning a fun day for the three of us. A picnic at the park for lunch, home for Oakley's nap, then over to his parents' for dinner.

I hadn't met them yet, but I'd heard this was a big step for him.

I was also going to meet his Uncle Doug, who'd been part of my rescue. He was the Chief of Police in Redlynne and had coordinated the pickup of Lydia and Calvin's bodies. He'd also busted up the whole gang after discovering who was behind it.

The old printing company had been a front for stolen goods and a warehouse for drugs. Uncle Doug explained how they'd funneled money from those sales back into their numerous businesses. Any business with significant cash flow worked best: bars, strip clubs, nail salons. They'd ring up fake drinks and food orders. Bogus inventory for products in their stores. It sounded so complicated, and I was sure I was missing details on how it all worked.

The biggest surprise from all of this had been seeing Hank and Cecil working together. I didn't know if they'd continue to work together, but it was nice to see their faces that day.

"I told you, little lady, you needed to stay out of trouble." Hank hugged me for the first time ever. "We almost lost you this time for real."

"Yeah, if your friend hadn't alerted us, you'd have been a goner for sure." Cecil chimed in.

"I'm just glad y'all found us."

Al and Eddie waited for their turns to talk to me that day too, each hugging me close and whispering love and support.

"Well, little girl, are you ready to go get dressed for the day?" Clint asked, waking me from my thoughts.

She said something that sounded like yes. He picked her up and carried her to her room. I could hear him singing to her and her trying to sing along with him.

It made me happy that he could be so accepting of her. Honestly, he had been when we'd dated before, but it was still nice to see.

Cate had wanted her daughter to have a better life than she'd had. She wanted two parents to love her, wanted her to have a home, a place to call hers. Oakley was lucky to have so many of those things, including a large extended family and friends. She even had her very own dog.

From my place on the couch, I could hear him in there making her laugh as he changed her. Once she was ready, he brought her back to me.

"Here she is." He leaned forward to give me a quick kiss. "I'm going to get dressed. Back in a jiff."

I watched Oakley trying to stand. It would be any day now. I wouldn't be surprised if she was walking by the time she was ten months old.

While I sat there, a ghost appeared. Calvin. I jumped nearly off the sofa, but my leg prevented it.

"Calvin?"

"Hi Jo," he said sheepishly.

"What're you doing here?"

"I'm sorry. I hate to barge in, but I just wanted to apologize to you." He paused. "I shouldn't have let it go that far. I didn't think... I didn't think she was capable of that."

I didn't know what to say to him. He'd always been nice to me, yet he'd helped her with my kidnapping and stood by while she nearly shot me. Still, I thought he'd felt trapped by her and didn't know how to get away.

"I appreciate you coming here. I don't really know what else to say."

"I understand. What can you say? I should have stood up for you, for Ted, for myself."

"Have you spoken to Ted since...?"

"Once. I told him it was us. He didn't take it well, but he was also upset that you were involved like that. I don't know if he'll forgive me, but I do not forgive Lydia for any of this."

I nodded because I didn't trust myself to speak.

"Well, I'll let you get back to your life. Again, I'm sorry." He waved and was gone.

He'd always been a man of few words, and in fact, that was the most I'd really heard him speak. With those words, though, I finally felt the closure I'd been seeking. It took Calvin's words to heal my heart.

At that moment, Clint came into the room, flashing me his oh-so-handsome grin. He healed me in many different ways too, and in turn, I hoped I'd helped in his healing process.

"Are my ladies ready for a picnic at the park?"

"We are."

His ladies. That felt good to hear.

Before you go: If you loved Organized Murder and haven't already received a copy of Unsolved Murder, the prequel to this series check out my website for the offer for your free novella.

www.ejwheltonwrites.com

Note by the Author:

Thank you for once again reading my stories. I have to say I love this series so much. The characters are with me daily, and they have become some of my best friends in a strange, pretend way. I hope that I am bringing them to life for you as well.

I have so many people to thank, but there are just too many. I'm afraid if I start naming, I will leave someone out and hurt someone's feelings. That's never my intention.

I have the most wonderful friends and family that have been supporting me through this journey.

So, thank you so much to those who have helped in the big ways (my BETA Readers and editors). Thank you to those who have listened to my countless hours of talking about writing (but not writing). To those that have answered my numerous questions about everything from phrases to grammar, thank you. If you have given me any feedback, just know I appreciate it all.

I do want to apologize for how long it took me to get this one out. It has been nearly 10 months since I published Replicated Murder and now Organized Murder. Life happens. I am working hard so that my next book (yet to be named) will not take as long to get published. I have at least three more books planned for this series but hoping to keep it going even longer.

Stay tuned!

www.ingramcontent.com/pod-product-compliance
Lightning Source LLC
Chambersburg PA
CBHW021149190726
48288CB00008B/2903